PRAIRIE
LOTUS

E PARK

PRAIRIE LOTUS

CLARION BOOKS

HOUGHTON MIFFLIN HARCOURT

BOSTON   NEW YORK

Clarion Books
3 Park Avenue
New York, New York 10016

Clarion Books is an imprint of Houghton Mifflin Harcourt Publishing Company.

hmhbooks.com

The text was set in Goudy Old Style.

Book design by Andrea Miller

Library of Congress Cataloging-in-Publication Data

Names: Park, Linda Sue, author.
Title: Prairie lotus / Linda Sue Park.
Description: Boston ; New York : Clarion Books, Houghton Mifflin Harcourt,
[2020] | Summary: In Dakota Territory in the 1880s, part-Asian Hanna and
her white father face racism and resistance to change as they try to make
a home for themselves. Includes author's note.
Identifiers: LCCN 2019007372 | ISBN 9781328781505 (hardcover)
Subjects: | CYAC: Racially mixed people—Fiction. | Frontier and pioneer
life—Dakota Territory—Fiction. | Fathers and daughters—Fiction. |
Racism—Fiction. | Dressmaking—Fiction. | Dakota Territory—Fiction.
Classification: LCC PZ7.P22115 Pr 2020 | DDC [Fic]—dc23
LC record available at https://lccn.loc.gov/2019007372

ISBN: 978-0-358-36014-8 (signed edition)

Manufactured in the United States of America
DOC 10 9 8 7 6 5 4 3 2 1
4500789009

To all those whose stories have
been erased or
silenced in the past:
May your stories sing and shape
and color the future.

PRAIRIE
LOTUS

Dakota Territory
April 1880

———— ❦ ————

"Should be our last day," Papa said when they stopped to make camp. He unhitched the tired horses from the wagon, then led them down a little draw to water, while Hanna began clearing the ground for a fire.

They had journeyed for almost a month since leaving Cheyenne, their most recent stretch in near three years of travel. Three years without a real home. Tomorrow they would reach their destination: LaForge, a railroad town in Dakota Territory.

Hanna was looking forward to cooking supper. They had been able to buy groceries in North Platte, but since then, it had rained for almost a solid week. They'd had to make do with meal after meal of stale biscuit and cold beans.

She had put dried codfish to soak the night before. *Soup*, she thought. *With onions and potatoes.*

Papa returned with the horses and a bucket of water. He fastened the horses to their picket lines, then left again to gather some brushwood.

"I'm going to make soup," she told him when he returned to start the fire.

"About time we had a hot meal," he said.

Hanna bristled at the note of petulance in his voice; the dreary weather of the past week was hardly her fault. But she said nothing, not wanting to start a row.

"Sky's clearing," he said. "Maybe it'll be easier to scare up a rabbit or something." He went off with his gun on his arm, his long-legged strides covering ground quickly.

Hanna watched him until he vanished behind a low rise. The endless prairie looked flat at first glance, but the land was never completely level. Rain had rinsed the gray and beige plains, leaving behind a translucence of green that was growing denser every day.

She went into the wagon and opened her trunk. She took out a piece of plain brown wrapping paper, a pencil, a rubber eraser, and a well-worn magazine.

The paper had been folded accordion-style several times and folded across twice. Opened out, the creases formed rectangles about two inches wide and three inches tall—three dozen of them.

Hanna had used up about half the rectangles on one side of the paper. In each was a small pencil sketch of a dress. Housedresses, visiting dresses, dresses for church, even ball gowns. She had seen pictures of ball gowns in the *Godey's Lady's Book* magazine, and it was fun to draw the elegant garments, even though she would never have a chance to see or wear one.

Now she leafed through an issue of *Godey's* from last summer, the latest she had been able to get. On page after page, there were drawings of every kind of garment. Some were available ready-made; for others, paper patterns and instructions could be mail-ordered.

She found pictures of two gowns that interested her. She took up her pencil and began to draw, combining the bodice of one dress with the skirt of the other. She also added a trimming of braid around the cuffs and hem of the bodice.

She eyed the drawing critically. Something wasn't quite

right. The skirt was too full for the length of the bodice. She erased the skirt and drew it again, this time with a slimmer profile.

Yes. Better.

For the past three years, Hanna had done all the family sewing. Papa bought his coats and jackets; she made his trousers, overalls, shirts, drawers, and nightshirts, as well as her own dresses and undergarments. Using paper patterns that had belonged to Mama, she knew how to adjust measurements to the correct size. She could backstitch, whipstitch, sew buttonholes; when she hemmed a garment or added trimming, her stitches were nearly invisible. With all that experience behind her, she was confident that she could make a dress of her own design, and she intended to try very soon.

She loved sketching because it took all her attention; she could stop thinking about the rest of the world for a while. As for sewing, most of the time it was both soothing and satisfying. She hadn't been able to draw or sew for several weeks now; riding in the wagon, it was too bumpy for fine work, and by the time they stopped to camp, it was almost always too dark.

Before long, she had to put away her drawing things to cook supper. She lifted the three-legged cast-iron spider from its hook on one of the wagon bows; it was deep enough to make soup for two people. Spider in hand, she jumped to the ground, took a few steps, and stopped in mid-stride.

A group of Indians stood in a loose semicircle between the wagon and the fire.

Hanna had seen Indians from the wagon several times, but always at a distance. At such moments, Papa seemed watchful but not particularly worried. He told her that the government had forced the Indians in this region, most of them members of the Sioux tribe, off the wide-open prairie and onto tracts of land reserved for them. They were not allowed to leave that land without special permission from the reservation's Indian agent.

Hanna looked over the group quickly. Three women, the eldest with gray-streaked hair. A girl a few years younger than Hanna, and two little girls. The women were wearing faded blankets or shawls. They carried cloth sacks or bundles; one had a baby tied to her back.

Mothers and daughters. Hanna thought at once of Mama. *What would she say or do if she were here?*

"Hello," she said. "I was just going to make soup. Would you like some?"

Mama had been a great believer in soup. She could conjure delicious soups from nothing but scraps and bones, and she had taught Hanna the secret: One strongly flavored ingredient could make the whole pot of leftovers tasty, and you didn't need much of it. Dried mushrooms, cabbage, and garlic were all good. So was dried fish.

Hanna used the big pot instead of the spider. She cut up the potatoes smaller than usual, so they would cook more quickly. The Indians sat on the ground near the fire. Hanna was anxious to serve them, but she forced herself to wait until the potatoes were properly cooked through.

She also found herself hoping that Papa wouldn't return anytime soon. *He might frighten them. Or maybe the other way round.*

Hanna had enough spoons for her guests, but only four bowls. The oldest of the Sioux women seemed to be the group's leader, so Hanna served her first. She glanced down at the soup in her bowl, then looked up, pursed her lips, and motioned with her chin toward Hanna.

Hanna understood at once. *She wants to be sure that I eat too.*

She filled two more bowls and handed them out for the rest of the group to share. The fourth bowl was for herself. She sat on the wagon steps to eat, near the group but not with them.

The women talked quietly among themselves.

—Oyu'l waste

—Sku'ya sni

—Nina ota mnisku'ya kte hchin

Hanna wondered what they were saying, but at least she could tell that they were enjoying the soup. After the oldest woman tasted it, she said something to the others. Then another woman had a bite and said something else. They each took a second taste and had further conversation. It was just like Mama's friends in Chinatown, or the lady visitors at Miss Lorna's boardinghouse: They were talking about the soup—the ingredients, the flavors.

By the end of the meal, the two little girls had grown brave enough to draw closer to Hanna. When she smiled at them, they shrieked in delight and ran back to the others.

The women rose to leave. Their leader addressed Hanna.

—Wahan'pi kin nina waste, na pidamaya

Her voice was quiet as she nodded at Hanna. Hanna nodded back, hoping it was the right response.

Mama always gave guests food to take home. She turned and hurried to the wagon, found an empty flour sack, and put in a few fistfuls of dried beans, then returned to her guests. She handed the sack to the gray-haired elder.

The old woman turned and had a brief exchange with her companions. One of them reached into her bundle, pulled something out, and passed it to the leader. She held it at shoulder height; it dangled from her hand.

It looked like a string of small white onions, or perhaps bulbs of garlic, braided together by their stems.

The old woman nodded at Hanna, then said something that sounded like "timp-sina." She gave the braid a little shake.

"Timp-sina?" Hanna repeated hesitantly.

The little girls giggled, and the women smiled.

"Timpsina," Hanna said again, this time with more certainty.

The old woman gave the braid to Hanna, who examined it with interest. The white tubers were clearly some kind of vegetable. The largest, at the bottom, were as big as a child's fist. They tapered in size along the length of the braid, the smallest about the size of a walnut. She touched one of them. It was rock hard.

They've been dried, like Mama used to do with mushrooms.

She looked up to see the old woman watching her closely. The woman pursed her lips again; this time she jerked her chin toward the kettle on the fire.

It's as if she's pointing with her lips, Hanna thought. "I cook them in water?" she asked. She pointed at the kettle.

Shaking her head, the woman motioned toward the kettle again, and then toward the sky, tracing the path of the sun from east to west. She held up three fingers.

"Three days?" Hanna said. *She can't possibly mean to cook them for three days. Kettle — water —*

"Oh! I should soak them for three days, before I cook them?" She made appropriate gestures as she spoke.

The old woman smiled and nodded. Then she waved toward one of the empty soup bowls.

"Soak for three days and then use them in soup?"

At that, the other women broke into murmurs of agreement, and the leader nodded again approvingly.

"Thank you," Hanna said. "Thank you for the—the timpsina."

The whole group laughed, and Hanna grinned at them.

As the Indians departed, one of the little girls turned her head to stare at Hanna. Her eyes were very dark, almost black, and at the same time, bright with curiosity.

Hanna and the girl looked at each other for a long time, until the Indians disappeared beyond a rise in the prairie.

Papa returned without any game. Hanna told him about the visitors.

"Indians?" he said with a frown.

"Women and girls," she said quickly. "They gave me this." She showed him the braid.

"Prairie turnip," he said. "Seen it before, in Kansas."

"What do they taste like?"

Papa thought for a moment. "Half turnip, half potato. Tasty enough, as I recall." A pause. "Good thing you fed them. Wouldn't want any trouble."

Hanna let a moment go by; she didn't want to sound impudent. "Not even a hint of trouble, Papa."

"You can't be too careful when they don't keep their distance," he countered. "Minnesota, the Black Hills—we're smack in the middle between the two."

She knew what Papa was talking about. For years there

had been bloody skirmishes between the Indians and white people. Like many other tribes, the Sioux had signed a treaty with the US government, promising that white settlers would not encroach on Indian land. Every single treaty had been broken—by settlers, or the government, or both.

"I don't blame them for fighting back," Hanna said. "It's just not fair."

"That's not the point," Papa said. He made a wide sweep with his arm, almost a full circle. "Most of the land around here used to be part of the Great Sioux Reservation. They left it as it was, all wild and unfarmed, so why shouldn't folks settle there? The land ought to go to people who work to improve it. That means farming, railroads, businesses. Churches. Schools. You want those things, you gotta have somewhere to build 'em."

Hanna did want those things; she especially wanted to go to school. She wondered why it wasn't possible for whites and Indians to share the land somehow. But she already knew from living in California that most white people didn't like having neighbors—Chinese, Indians, Mexicans—who weren't white themselves.

Hanna wrapped the prairie turnips in a clean feed sack.

Her next thought surprised her. *They all had black hair. I haven't seen so many people with black hair since we left China-town in Salt Lake.*

She drew in a long breath. *And there won't be any where we're going, either.*

As Papa drove the wagon up the wide main street, Hanna rose from her seat at the back and peeked around the edge of the canvas cover. She saw packed-dirt streets and buildings of raw lumber identified by hand-lettered signs: a dry-goods store, a hardware store, a saloon, a feed store. There was even a furniture shop, a rarity in these hinterlands.

It seems like a nice enough place.

Wishful thinking, maybe. LaForge was little different from the other frontier towns she had seen: the railroad at the north end, with Main Street at a right angle to it, leading to the livery at the south end. A brand-new town, equal measures of promise and uncertainty, like the thin April sunshine in which it stood.

The hotel was near the depot. Papa got them a room for the night. Hanna climbed the stairs along the outside of the building carrying a valise and a sack atop a wooden box. With her bonnet tied on firmly and the load piled high in her arms, her face was mostly hidden from view.

Papa followed her into the room with his own valise. "All right?" he asked.

She set her belongings down and nodded.

He went to the window and pulled the curtain across. "Livery next," he said. "I won't be long." He would take their horses, Chester the roan and Cherry the sorrel mare, to be boarded at the livery, and park the wagon there too.

He didn't have to tell her to stay away from the window, out of sight. She knew what to do, after so many months and so many towns. Papa always thought it best that he acquaint himself with a few folks and set up either a dry-goods or a tailoring business before people found out about her.

And same as always, she couldn't stop herself from hoping: Maybe this would be the last move for her and Papa, the last time she would have to hide her face on arriving in a new town.

She closed the door behind him and turned the key in

the lock. Then she crossed the room and put the wooden box on the bed. Work would make the time go faster.

Mama's button box was one of the few things from the shop in Los Angeles that had made the long journey with them. During the trip, the box had been joggled and jostled and overturned completely more than once. She unlatched the little hook, lifted the lid, and saw what she had suspected: buttons all jumbled together willy-nilly.

"Rotten eggs," she muttered, using Mama's favorite curse.

Papa had made the box to Mama's design. It was a rectangular tray covered with a hinged lid and fitted with a wooden grid that divided the space inside into dozens of compartments. The largest button box Hanna had ever seen, it held the hundreds of buttons that Mama had collected for years.

Hanna cherished the button box because it had belonged to Mama. Every inch of space in the wagon was needed for traveling essentials, so most of Mama's things had been left behind. And her most prized possession—an enormous mirror fixed to the wall—could not be moved at all. Hanna had managed to rescue the button box and Mama's favorite woolen shawl, brown with a red plaid pattern.

Hanna emptied the buttons onto the bed. She began by digging through the pile and putting one button into each compartment. Rows by size. Columns by color. The square in the lower left corner contained the smallest white button. Above it, she put the next size, also white. Each square held a bigger button until she reached the top left, which held the largest white button.

In the next column she put cream-colored buttons. Then beige, shades of brown, gray, black. After that came the rainbow colors, red, orange, yellow, shades of green and blue, and finally violet. Several more columns and rows held novelty buttons, shaped like animals or stars or cherries.

The buttons were pretty to look at and pleasantly smooth under her fingertips. The orderliness of each button in its proper place was soothing. Best of all, sorting the buttons kept her occupied.

She put the last few buttons in their compartments, then closed the lid and latched it. She ran her finger over the carving on the lid, a simple five-petaled lotus. Mama's favorite flower. It was her trademark: She would use tiny lazy-daisy stitches to embroider a lotus in the lining of every garment she made, and she had taught Hanna to do the same. Hanna had never actually seen a lotus plant, but

Mama had shown it to her in Chinese paintings and on ceramic vases.

Hanna still had the first little lotus flower she had ever embroidered. Pressed carefully into the Bible Miss Lorna had given her when they left Los Angeles was a square of plain muslin with two lotuses: one done by Mama as an example, and the other by seven-year-old Hanna. Mama's stitches were even, symmetrical, with perfect tension. Those by Hanna were wobbly and uncertain. But Mama had praised her effort, and since then, Hanna had embroidered a lotus countless times, always striving to make hers as even and graceful as Mama's.

Hanna was putting away the button box when Papa's boots thudded on the stairs.

"Is there a school?" Hanna asked.

It was always her first question. Some of the towns they had passed through didn't have a school yet. Those that did, they hadn't stayed in long enough for her to enroll.

Papa took off his hat and hung it on a nail near the door. He was tall and lean, and his knees and elbows jutted out when he sat on the room's only chair. "Forgot to ask," he said. "I had more important things on my mind. I'll give you the bad news first. There are already two dry-goods stores, a tailor, and a shirtmaker here in town."

She knew why it was bad news. No town this size needed *three* dry-goods stores. Or two shirtmakers.

Now Papa was almost-not-quite smiling. "Two dry-goods stores plus a furniture store? That tells me there are already plenty of women here."

During the endless months of travel from Los Angeles to LaForge, Hanna and Papa had passed through town after town populated largely by menfolk. The farther west on the frontier, the fewer the women. In traveling east, Hanna and Papa had finally reached country where more women were living.

Hanna realized what Papa was saying. "There's no dressmaker!" she exclaimed.

"I signed a one-month lease for a building on Second Street, and I bought the last vacant lot on Main. We'll get a shop built and set up to sell dress goods."

"And make dresses," she said, her voice edged with defiance.

They had argued about this before. It had been fine when she was just a helper, at the shop in Los Angeles, but

Papa thought that at fourteen, she was too young for the full responsibility of making dresses for grown women.

He went on as if she hadn't spoken. "The drugstore's on one side and a general store on the other. There'll be plenty of traffic on that part of the street."

"That sounds fine, Papa," she said.

She would keep quiet for now, but she was already scheming to change his mind.

"You bought the lot?" she asked, trying to make her words sound like simple curiosity.

"You questioning my decision?" His voice rose in querulousness that she knew could easily become anger.

"No, Papa," she said firmly, looking him in the eye. It was true: Papa had his faults, but he was a shrewd businessman. "I'm just wondering, why now? Why this place?" Since selling the shop in Los Angeles, they had always lived and worked in rented buildings.

He nodded; the glint of anger in his eyes faded slowly. "A couple of reasons. First, because of Harris."

A man named Philip Harris was the reason that Hanna and Papa had come to Dakota. Papa had met him years earlier, in Kansas. At the end of last winter, when they decided to leave Cheyenne, Papa heard that Mr. Harris was justice of the peace in LaForge. "A good man," Papa had said. "A fair man. Might as well go there as anywhere else."

"He'll do his best to see that we get a fair shake here," he went on. "I'm figuring on giving it until fall. If the shop doesn't do well, we can sell up and move on. There'll be plenty of buyers, town right on the railroad and growing fast."

Hanna nodded, more than satisfied. *Until fall. That's time enough for at least one, maybe even two terms of school.*

As a young man, barely out of his teens, Papa had left his home in Tennessee to travel west, and eventually ended up in Colorado Territory during the Gold Rush near Pike's Peak. He had worked hard and been lucky, doing very well for himself. When the rush was over, he took a job as a supplier for the railroad. He kept moving, finally reaching Los Angeles, where he couldn't go any farther west, and set up as a trader dealing mostly in dry goods.

A year or so later, he met Mama, and they fell in love.

It should have been a simple story. But it wasn't.

Because Mama was Chinese.

Orphaned as a toddler in China, Mama had been

taken in by American missionaries. Her Chinese name was Mei Li; the missionaries called her May. They taught her to sew, and to read and write as well. She grew up entranced by their books and the stories of their homeland. When she was eighteen, she convinced them to let her make the journey to the land that was by then known as Gam Saan—Gold Mountain.

One of the missionaries had a sister who ran a boardinghouse in Los Angeles. That was where May stayed when she first arrived in America, with Miss Lorna. She cleaned house, helped with the meals, took in sewing.

Then a young man came to board at Miss Lorna's place. He was setting up a dry-goods shop just outside Chinatown, and he needed a seamstress.

May went to work for the young man, whose name was Ben.

Papa.

The riots in Los Angeles happened when Hanna was five years old. By then they were living above the shop. She wasn't old enough to understand, but she was plenty old enough to remember.

Shouts in the street.

Someone pounding on the door.

More shouting.

"Take her. To Miss Lorna's," Mama said to Papa.

"You go—you can both stay there," Papa said.

"No. You. Safer with you."

Papa held Hanna's hand and pulled her through streets filled with people running, shouting, screaming. The air smelled strongly of smoke. Sometimes Papa picked her up and ran, dodging crowds of people who looked angry or frightened or both.

He left her with Miss Lorna. "I'll be back for her as soon as I can," he said, over Hanna's head.

"I'll keep her as long as you need," Miss Lorna said. "You're not to worry about her."

Hanna stayed at Miss Lorna's for what felt like forever. But it was really only a few days before Papa returned.

The news was bad. At least fifteen Chinese men had been lynched. Chinese-owned houses and businesses had been ransacked, looted, burned. While Papa stood guard at his shop, Mama had gone to check on her friends. In trying to help them save their noodle shop, she had been overcome by smoke and collapsed.

Papa brought her home. He and Hanna nursed her as best they could, but her lungs were badly damaged. The sounds of her coughing, wheezing, and gasping filled the house every hour, day and night. Each cough made Hanna flinch, imagining the pain her mother was feeling, the constant desperate strain for something as simple as air.

Mama struggled for six years after that. On a cold rainy morning in February, a few months before Hanna's twelfth birthday, a thick silence woke her. She got out of bed and saw that the door to her parents' room was ajar. She peeked around the edge of the door.

Mama was lying on a quilt on the floor. She was curled up on her side, and Hanna could see her face, so calm and sweet that she was almost smiling.

Sitting on the edge of the bed in his nightshirt, Papa cleared his throat, then looked up and saw Hanna. "She must have gotten out of bed in the middle of the night," he said. "She didn't wake me—I never felt or heard a thing."

Hanna tiptoed into the room and sat down at the foot of the bed.

"Where your mama came from, a lot of people sleep on the floor," he said. "Only rich people have beds."

Hanna's eyes were watering; she wiped away the tears with the sleeve of her nightgown. "Is that what she was doing, Papa? Sleeping the way she used to?"

"Partly. Maybe. But I think she knew somehow that the end was coming, and she didn't want . . . She knew that no one likes to sleep in a bed where someone has died." He shook his head. "Always had to be thinking of someone else. And look where it got her."

Hanna hoped that the anger in his voice was just his way of sorrowing. She concentrated on looking at Mama's face. *So peaceful. Her last present to me, to know she was at peace when—when the end came.* The wave of grief that swept over Hanna receded a little when she realized that the terrible wheezing sounds had stopped at last.

Three weeks later, Papa sold the shop and bought a wagon. They packed up and left to search for a place to live that would be free of Mama's ghost, the memory of her sickness, her death, and the riot that had eventually killed her.

ON THEIR SECOND DAY in LaForge, they moved from the hotel into the rented house. The first thing they did was hang curtains so no one would be able to see inside. Then Papa went off to the lumberyard, leaving Hanna to unpack.

Only a few minutes after he left, she heard the thump of what sounded like dozens of feet on the board sidewalk. She hurried to the window and twitched the curtain back just enough to see.

Five young boys were running and calling out to one another. They turned the corner and went down Second Street. Behind them, three little girls followed more sedately. Those children, all headed in the same direction first thing in the morning? They had to be going to school.

Hanna had never been to school. She had learned her letters and numbers from Mama, and then she'd had lessons with Miss Lorna. When she and Papa left Los Angeles, Miss Lorna had given her a whole set of readers, a grammar, a speller, and an arithmetic. Hanna had worked her way through all of them diligently. But she'd had no one to teach her. And Mama had always wanted her to go to school.

"My smart girl. Finish school and get your diploma. Studying trains your mind, makes it stronger."

Hanna stomped into the kitchen. She cleaned up the breakfast dishes and put a kettle of water on the stove to heat. Once the water was hot, she dumped it into the tin dishpan so she could clean the floor. She swept and scrubbed, feeling more determined by the moment.

Papa came in for the noon meal, took one look at her face, and said, "Whatever it is, you wait until after we've eaten. I'll not have you spoiling my appetite."

They chewed their beans and biscuit in silence. As they ate, she felt the heat of her agitation cooling into something steadier and more solid. *A tree stump. No, a rock. A big boulder that takes a yoke of oxen to move.*

Her thoughts were running away a little. She got up to

fetch the teakettle and poured two cups. Papa stirred in a spoon of sugar and took a sip.

"Good biscuit," he said.

"Thank you." Pause. "There's school here."

He gulped his tea. "You don't say."

"Papa."

"What do you need to go to school for? You can read and write and figure, you'll never need more than that."

"I want to graduate."

"Nothing but a piece of paper. I didn't graduate, hasn't hurt me any."

"It wouldn't take long. I've finished the Sixth Reader. One term, maybe two, that's all."

"Hanna, we can't have any attention called to us," he snapped. "Your going to school could maybe cause a ruckus. That's the last thing we need."

A moment's silence.

"Mr. Harris," she said.

"Harris? What's he got to do with anything?"

"If he's justice of the peace, doesn't that mean—couldn't he stop any trouble—"

"That's what I'm talking about! You cause trouble and we'll never be able to make a success in this town, you know that!" Papa was shouting now. She figured that she had one last chance before he stopped listening altogether.

"Mama wanted me to graduate."

She held her breath. Sometimes mentioning Mama helped . . . but not always. Papa had often clashed with Mama, even toward the end, when she could speak only a few words between snatched breaths. Hanna had inherited a good bit of Mama's stubbornness, as well as her straight black hair, tan skin, dark curved eyes.

He stared down into his teacup. "She wanted a lot of things," he mumbled.

"Things she could never have. This one, I can still do for her."

At last he looked up, glaring. "Funny you should mention Harris," he said. "Turns out he's on the school board as well. So he's the one I'll have to speak to. But I'm not making any promises, you hear?"

"Yes. Thank you, Papa."

She fetched the kettle and freshened his tea.

Hanna realized too late that she hadn't gotten Papa to promise *when* he would speak to Mr. Harris. She wanted to start school right away, but by the end of the week, no more had been said about it. A dozen times she'd had to bite her tongue to keep from asking. She knew that if he felt she was nagging, he might change his mind about the whole thing.

He's been busy, she told herself yet again. He was spending his days at the depot, the lumberyard, the hardware store, buying and ordering and hauling supplies for the building of the shop.

Hanna was busy as well. A pile of clothes to be mended waited on one chair, with an even bigger pile of laundry on another. At her request, Papa had brought her lengths of muslin from one of the dry-goods stores to make bed linens. She couldn't wait to sleep in clean new sheets after so many grubby nights in the wagon.

All that had to wait, though. First she needed to sieve the flour and the cornmeal. She found the box that held the sifter, a ring of tin with a mesh bottom, and brought out the flour sack. A few cupfuls at a time, she poured flour into the sifter and shook it over her largest cooking pot. The flour fell through the mesh, leaving behind an assortment of weevils, pantry moths, and flour worms. After she finished, she went outside to empty the sieve by flinging the insects into the yard. The sieved flour went into a big crock with a good tight lid. No pests could get into the crock; it would stay free of bugs, provided she made sure it held only clean flour.

It took a while to sieve all the flour. Then Hanna had to repeat the whole process with the bag of cornmeal. For a brief moment as she shook the sieve, she wondered how she would ever get all the work done once she was in school—it was hard enough when she had the whole day.

Before she was sick, Mama used to work in the shop all day, and she still kept house. Their Los Angeles home hadn't been perfect, but they'd always had hot food and clean clothes, and that was more than plenty. Hanna was determined to do the same.

Hanna sat up very straight, hands folded in her lap, feet drawn in beneath her skirt. Any moment now, Mr. Harris would be calling.

"I've already talked to him some," Papa had told her that morning. "I mentioned that Mama was Chinese."

"What did he say?"

Papa shrugged. "Not much. Something like, 'Well now, I wasn't expecting that.'"

Hanna felt her spirits lift a little and immediately tamped them down. It wasn't a nasty response, but then again, it could mean almost anything. She had spent the day wondering what she should say to Mr. Harris, rehearsing different lines in her head. In a moment of panic, she had fetched her arithmetic book to go over decimals. Maybe he would ask her questions about her grade levels, and arithmetic was her weakest subject. But after a few minutes, she put the book away. If she didn't know it well by now, she was not going to be able to learn it in an afternoon.

She tidied up quickly after supper, took off her apron, and redid her braid. Then she sat in the chair next to the lamp table and coaxed herself into stillness. Mama had taught her that—how to sit still and breathe deeply when she was feeling especially twitchy or distressed.

All the same, she jumped when a knock sounded on the door.

Mr. Harris came in and took off his hat. He had a full brown beard and very blue eyes. He greeted Papa with a handshake. The two men sat down opposite her.

She sensed Mr. Harris's response on seeing her for the first time. The quick glance, the even quicker look away, unspoken curiosity clouding the air. Hanna hadn't made up her mind if this was better or worse than when people just plain stared at her.

"Would you like coffee or tea, Mr. Harris?" Hanna asked. Her voice trembled a little, but she managed to steady it.

"No, thank you," he said. Again, Hanna recognized the kind of astonishment she'd perceived before in so many other people. *She speaks, she speaks English, she speaks English politely!*

But already she could see what Papa had meant when he called Mr. Harris a fair man. Mr. Harris had answered her as if she were anyone else, keeping his surprise silent. That was far more than most people managed. Some busted out with something rude or hurtful or even hateful. Most others spoke to Papa as if she weren't there.

Papa and Mr. Harris chatted for a few more minutes. Hanna learned that the Harrises had a son named James who had moved to Oregon the previous fall.

"I wanted to go too," Mr. Harris said. "But I'd promised Sarah Lynn that this would be our last move. So we stayed, and James went on with my brother's family."

"Heard it's pretty country out there," Papa said.

"Not settled up yet, though, and Sarah Lynn wanted the girls to go to school. Speaking of school . . ." He looked at Hanna, then back at Papa. "I've been thinking on this.

Edmunds, you're already contributing to the local economy, and you don't seem like the type to skip out on your tax bill."

Papa grinned. "That'll depend on how big it is," he said, and the men laughed together. Hanna smiled, silently wishing they would get on with the conversation.

Then Mr. Harris grew serious. "The way I see it, any child under the age of twenty-one resident in the town of LaForge has the right to attend school here. I'll tell Miss Walters to expect a new student on Monday." Pause. "Thing is, we don't want any . . . trouble. The school needs to run smoothly, and if anything gets in the way of that, Miss Walters will be the one making the decisions."

"That's fair enough," Papa said.

No, Hanna thought at once. *It's not fair. Even if I do everything right, I've got no say over what the other students might do.*

"Any questions?" Mr. Harris asked.

She looked down at her hands in her lap for a long moment, then raised her head. "I haven't been lucky enough to go to school before, Mr. Harris," she said, "so I'm sorry I don't know this already. Are students allowed to keep their hats on in the schoolroom?"

THE SCHOOLHOUSE STOOD BY ITSELF in an empty stretch of prairie, the only building on Second Street west of Main. From afar, it looked as if it were barely afloat on the expanse of rolling grassland. As Hanna drew nearer, she could see the lean-to tacked to the north wall, a miniature of the structure itself, its peaked roof copying the angle of the main roof.

Hanna hesitated at the schoolhouse door, her head lowered. She stared at the weave of her blue cambric dress. The fabric was sturdy, made for everyday, but she had added rows of featherstitching to the cuffs and hem. Not showy, but not plain, either.

She had been up most of the night, dozing off for only

moments at a time, always waking with her heart pounding. At long last, she was getting the chance to go to school —and she found herself dreading it.

Images from her younger years appeared in her mind's eye. Children taunting her, shouting derisively in fake Chinese, pulling at the corners of their eyes to mock her. The few who spoke to her did so only on a dare: When she answered, they would screech in triumph and run back to their friends.

Their mothers were seldom better, and often worse. On spotting Hanna, they would cross the street hastily, sometimes covering their mouths as if she were diseased. Or they would pull their smaller children behind their skirts, protecting them. *From what?* Hanna always wondered.

As she stood on the threshold of the schoolhouse, it was hard for her to recall why she had wanted so badly to be here.

I could turn around and go home. Maybe Papa is right about a diploma being just a piece of paper . . .

Then Mama was in her head again, showing her how to weave the needle in and out of the last few stitches on the wrong side of a garment, pulling the thread through to ensure that the seam would not come unstitched.

"*Finish,*" Mama had said. "*Good work is no good if you don't finish.*"

A diploma was more than a piece of paper. It was proof that she had finished her high school studies.

A big breath. One arm wrapped tightly around her books and her face far back in a deep scoop bonnet, she turned the doorknob.

Hanna had deliberately arrived early; she wanted to be seated before the other students came in. The teacher, a fair young woman with light brown hair twisted into a knot low on the nape of her neck, was sitting behind a big desk across the room.

"You must be Hanna Edmunds," the teacher said. She did not smile, but her voice was kind. "I'm Miss Walters. I was told that you're fourteen, which would put you in the class with the oldest pupils. Have you started the Fifth Reader?"

"Yes, miss."

In fact, Hanna had already finished the *Sixth* Reader. She remembered the first time she had come across the poem titled "To My Mother." Her breath had caught hard enough to make her cough.

I know thou art gone to the land of thy rest . . .

Although Hanna knew well there were plenty of people who had lost their mothers, it had still stunned her to find a poem about a mother dying. It was as if the poet had seen right into her heart, and the poem immediately became her favorite. She thought of it as "Mama's poem."

But she didn't want to sound boastful about having already read the Sixth Reader, and besides, she loved the Fifth.

"Your desk is at the back there, on the left. You'll be sharing with Dolly Swenson."

"Thank you, miss."

Hanna made her way to the desk. She sat down, put her books away, and took out her reader. She bent over the book; the sides of the scoop bonnet kept her face all but hidden.

Mr. Harris had said that pupils usually took off their caps and bonnets, but that it was not actually a rule. He had agreed to tell Miss Walters that Hanna would wear her bonnet at school; the fact that she was half-Chinese would be kept from the other students until Hanna was ready for them to know.

"Just for a few days," Hanna had said to Mr. Harris.

Until I can make a friend. One friend.

Then she could take the bonnet off.

Miss Walters rang the bell, and for a few moments, the room was filled with the lively clatter of the other pupils. Hanna's seatmate slid in next to her. Hanna hated to be rude, but she didn't acknowledge the other girl's presence. It wasn't until Miss Walters called school to order that she risked a peek at Dolly.

Dolly was a strawberry blonde with skin as pale as bleached muslin. Hanna thought of what Mama had often said about pale skin: that it was considered desirable among Chinese people because it meant a life of privilege. "*You don't have to work outside. In sun, in wind. Only rich people, treasured wife, treasured daughter.*"

With that single glance, Hanna also appraised what Dolly was wearing: a dress of fine brown poplin that fit her nicely. But Hanna's practiced eye saw traces of picked-out seams along the bodice. Which meant that Dolly's dress had originally been a different size and had been made over for her.

She doesn't work outdoors, in the fields. Her family doesn't have enough money for new clothes, but she wants to dress nicely, so someone—her mother, probably—does the best she can with castoffs.

For most of her life, Hanna had made quick conclusions about the people she met, in an effort to guess how they might treat her. The trick was to keep her own conclusions light—never giving them too much weight, in case it turned out they were just plain wrong.

Is Dolly spoiled? Maybe.

The morning went by quickly enough. The teacher was tactful and did not call on Hanna to read or respond on her first day.

Miss Walters was a small woman; the oldest boys were all taller than she was. Her hair was styled with curled bangs; her dress was blue challis with a lace collar and cuffs. Very demure and proper, with one subtle exception: The bodice was buttoned with dark blue roundels made of sparkling cut glass.

Hanna knew that those buttons were costly. The button box held similar ones; she could picture the compartment, a third of the way down on the right-hand side. *Miss*

Walters—she chose them for her own pleasure. They're not too showy, but whenever she wants, she can look down and see them catch the light.

Somehow, Miss Walters reminded her a little of Mama. Maybe because Hanna wanted badly to see reminders of Mama and so seldom did.

At midday, most of the students went home for their noon meal. Hanna had brought her dinner pail because she did not want to walk through town with the other pupils on the way home to eat.

Two of the twenty children stayed and ate at their desks; Hanna guessed that they lived outside town on a homestead claim. Like the other towns in Dakota Territory, LaForge was surrounded by parcels of land, each 160 acres. People— usually men—would "claim" a parcel by filing their intention with the government and paying eighteen dollars. They had to farm the land and live on it half the year for five years, after which they had "proved" their claim and would own the land.

Hanna recalled the words of a popular folk song:
Uncle Sam is rich enough to give us all a farm!
Then she thought of the Indians she had met, and

wondered, as she often had before, why Uncle Sam was allowed to give away land that wasn't his in the first place.

Even though only two children remained at their desks for lunch, Hanna guessed that many of the other students lived on homestead claims as well. They would be staying in town for now, to go to school, and would move out to their claims when the term was finished.

As the hour came to an end, the older girls returned and gathered in the schoolroom. Having heard them recite their lessons earlier, Hanna now knew the names of the students in her class. Besides Dolly, the girls were Bess, Margaret, and Edith. Bess's last name was Harris, so she would be Mr. Harris's daughter. The boys were Albert, Ned, and Sam. Hanna guessed that Margaret and Albert were siblings—they looked so much alike.

Bess and Ned were the best students. Edith smiled the most.

Hanna sensed something else, too.

The other girls don't like Dolly.

Bess, Margaret, and Edith stood in a cluster at the window, watching the boys play ball outside, with Dolly standing a step apart. Hanna stayed at her desk, her reader open in front of her, although she wasn't reading. She was thinking.

The girls might not like Dolly because she's spoiled. So I could be right about that.

Or she could be perfectly nice, and they're mean to her for some other reason that might not be her fault.

It seemed to Hanna that there were always a hundred reasons for disliking people and not nearly as many for liking them. For the moment, it was looking as if Dolly might be her best chance at a friend.

That afternoon, Miss Walters chose a few of the older students to read aloud from the Fifth Reader. Hanna stared down at her book, following every word.

Dolly and Ned took their turns. Then the teacher called on Bess.

Bess had brown hair braided and coiled at the back of her head. From the size of the coil, Hanna could tell that when unbraided, Bess's hair would fall to at least her hips. She was the shortest of the big girls, sturdily built, with a round face and a chin dimple. She chose a poem called "Minot's Ledge," about a lighthouse keeper and the shipwreck of his son's boat.

Like spectral hounds across the sky,
　　The white clouds scud before the storm;
And naked in the howling night
　　The red-eyed lighthouse lifts its form.

Bess read beautifully, her voice rising and falling like the sea's waves. There was not a sound in the room as she reached the closing stanzas: Young Charlie, with the chestnut hair and hazel eyes—would he survive the storm?

The other pupils had abandoned any pretense of attending to their own studies. They were all staring wide-eyed at Bess. When she finished reading, the whole room seemed to heave a sigh. Hanna stole a quick glance at Miss Walters, who seemed to be trying not to smile.

She knows that everyone is listening, Hanna thought, *but that's what she wanted.*

"Nicely done, Bess," Miss Walters said.

Hanna saw Bess blink a few times, almost as if waking, then blush at the teacher's praise and lower her head a little.

Why, she's a bit shy. But not while she was reading.

Sam was next. Although he was not much taller than the other students, he looked to be the oldest in the class, with wide shoulders and a firm brow. He was blond and brown-eyed, his face tanned and hair bleached by the sun. He had a very quick smile that might have been called cheeky if it weren't so friendly. "'The Blind Men and the Elephant,'" he announced.

Sam had chosen one of Hanna's very favorite selections from the reader, a funny poem about six blind men and their mistaken assumptions about an elephant. By the third stanza, most of the pupils were hiding their giggles behind their hands; by the fifth, many were chuckling out loud.

"Hush," Miss Walters said. Her voice was stern, but she had that same smile behind her eyes. Everyone quieted down to listen to Sam recite the last verses.

> And so these men of Indostan
> Disputed loud and long,
> Each in his own opinion
> Exceeding stiff and strong,
> Though each was partly in the right,
> And all were in the wrong!

Hanna couldn't help but smile as the whole room burst into applause and laughter. Sam was not the least bit shy. He grinned and made an exaggerated bow.

"Sam," Miss Walters said, "you read very well, but please remember that modesty is always becoming."

"Yes, Teacher," Sam said.

"You may return to your seat."

As Sam passed Hanna's desk, he was still smiling.

Is he smiling at me?

Alarmed, she tried to draw back deeper into her bonnet. She did not want to be singled out.

Not even by a nice-looking boy with a friendly smile.

HANNA WALKED HOME after her first day of school. It was only a few blocks, but it felt like miles, her feet heavy, her head heavier. She had done nothing but sit at a desk all day. But the effort of worrying—what Miss Walters thought of her, whether the other students could see her face despite the scoop bonnet, how she would ever amass enough courage to take it off . . . It had all been more exhausting than she could have imagined.

Supper was ready when Papa came in from the building site. Hanna had made the batter for sourdough pancakes the evening before and left it to rest down cellar overnight. She fried slices of salt pork and cooked the cakes in the drippings, and made brown-sugar syrup as well. It was one of Papa's favorite meals. He might come up with a hundred reasons why she shouldn't go to school, but his evening meal would not be one of them.

"Everything all right today?" he asked as he forked up a bite from his second plateful of pancakes. He was hungry after a full day's work building the new shop.

Hanna chose her words carefully. "I might need to catch up a little in arithmetic. But I'm ahead in every other subject."

"Hmm," he said. He finished his food in silence. Then he looked at her closely. "Any trouble?"

She shook her head, knowing that her anxiety and discomfort weren't the kind of trouble Papa meant. He was asking about trouble with the other students—the sort that came about because she wasn't white.

If she were white, she wouldn't have to wear the bonnet.

If she were white, she wouldn't have to ask about attending school.

If she were white . . .

Hanna could recall only one time in her life when she had wanted to be white. Back in Los Angeles, when she was around four years old, she had seen an older girl whose blond hair was all ringlets and curls. Hanna had taken a skein of yellow wool from Mama's knitting basket and played with it in front of the big mirror on the shop wall, draping the yarn over her head as she stared at her reflection. She had been more interested in the curl than the color; she kept trying to twist and twirl the yarn into ringlets, so different from her own straight tresses.

Then Mama had seen what she was doing. Without a word, she took the wool away from Hanna. She brought out a hairbrush and a fine cord of red silk. After brushing Hanna's shoulder-length hair, she plaited it carefully, weaving in the silk cord, then wrapping and tying it at the bottom of the braid.

Standing behind Hanna at the mirror, Mama moved the braid to rest on Hanna's shoulder. Hanna saw the red silk cord against her black hair, both of them smooth and shining. From that moment on, Hanna never again wished for blond curls.

How she missed it, the feel of Mama's hands doing her hair.

If she were white, she wouldn't be Mama's daughter. And she wouldn't have the same understanding of the precious knowledge that Mama had revealed to her a few weeks before she died.

"I'm half-half too. Just like you."

Hanna didn't know a single person besides herself who was half-Chinese and half-white. Mama always said it made her special. When she was younger, some things about being half-half did seem gratifying. Their dinner might be bread or potatoes—or rice or noodles, Chinese style. There were always two kinds of tea, green and black. Hanna could speak both Chinese and English.

Papa knew some Chinese—way more than most white people—but Mama's English had been better than his Chinese. So as a family, they had always spoken English. When it was just Hanna and Mama on their own, they usually spoke Chinese. But Hanna had not spoken Chinese for more than a year now, since leaving Salt Lake City's Chinatown. Sometimes she felt that she could almost see her Chinese slipping away, the words flitting around the edges of her memory and then flying off one by one.

Most of the time, being half-Asian and half-white was special in a hurtful way. White people, except for Miss Lorna and a few of her church friends, didn't like Hanna because she wasn't white. Chinese people accepted her but didn't like Papa because he *was*. Hanna's Chinese half was what Mama had given her. How could she ever wish that away? But why did her being half-and-half bother other people so much?

Then she learned that Mama, too, was half-and-half.

At the time, Mama's lungs were so bad that she was spending most of the day wrapped in the brown and red plaid shawl and huddled in the rocking chair. When she spoke, she had to strain for mouthfuls of air between words. Hanna recalled what Mama had said without those painful gaps.

"China is big, very big. Chinese people are all different, north, south, mountain people, river people, rice people, noodle people. Americans don't know this. They think all Chinese are the same."

Mama told Hanna stories about China. About temples and palaces with roofs of gold. About rice that grew in water up to its knees, the greenest green you could ever imagine. About dragons and phoenixes, emperors and princesses, jade and pearls.

Family stories, too. Hanna learned about her grandmother, Mama's mother, who could embroider flowers and butterflies that you would swear were alive. And her grandfather, a merchant who traveled hundreds of miles every year to gather and sell a precious plant.

"*Yansam*," Mama said. She asked for paper and pencil, then wrote a Chinese word and showed it to Hanna. "*It looks like a man, head, arms, legs. Grows like a potato.*"

"*In the ground?*" Hanna asked. "*Like a root?*"

"*Root, yes. For medicine.*"

Mama pulled the shawl more tightly around her. "*Listen,*" she said. "*I never told you this. My papa? He was not Chinese. He came to China from another place. A beautiful place, a secret place. Called Korea. Americans don't know that place.*"

Hanna frowned, thinking hard. "*It's another country?*"

"*Yes.*"

"*So your mama was Chinese, but your papa—*"

"*Yes. Korean.*" Mama smiled at her. "*I'm half-half too. Just like you.*"

Then she told Hanna some Korean stories. About the rabbit who lived in the moon, the turtle in the Sea King's palace. How it was Koreans who had invented chopsticks and made the most beautiful pottery in the world. Mama didn't know very many Korean words; she had spoken Chinese with her parents. But she was still proud of being half-Korean.

"*Your name is Hanna because of your grandmother,*" Mama said, "*your white grandmother.*"

51

Hanna knew that. Papa's mother, who lived in Tennessee — her name was Hannah.

"But for another reason, too. In Korean, ha-na means one." Mama held up her index finger. *"First daughter. Best, number-one daughter."*

She wrote another Chinese character. *"Girl, like me. Half-half, like me. This character means 'double happiness.' That's you. You are my double happiness."*

That memory was an enormous comfort to Hanna — one that she would take with her to school the next day.

When Hanna approached the schoolhouse in the morning, the oldest boys were playing catch in the yard while the younger pupils watched. The biggest girls were likely inside already.

I'm one of the big girls. So I ought to go in.

Hanna's steps slowed. Such a struggle, when something as simple as going into a building made her heart pound and her stomach twist. But she forced herself to take another step, and another, and still another, until at last she was over the threshold and in the lean-to, which served as an entry to the schoolroom. The lean-to had shelves and a double row of pegs along two of its walls, with the coal bin in one corner, empty now except for a layer of coal dust.

The schoolroom door was cracked open. Hanna heard voices on the other side.

"—think of any other reason?"

"It's by far the simplest. And the most logical. It just makes sense!"

The second voice was Dolly's. The first one, maybe Margaret's.

"I don't see the use of guessing." That was Bess.

"Oh, fiddle!" Dolly again. "It's her own fault for wearing it—she must have known it would make people wonder. And if it's not a horrible birthmark, it's probably some kind of nasty scar."

Hanna went stone-still. They were talking about *her*, wondering why she hadn't taken off her bonnet the day before.

Her head down, she stared at the books in her arms. The hem of her sleeve was turned up a little, revealing the tiny lotus she had embroidered there.

Not what I planned. I wanted to make at least one friend first. Rotten eggs—it'll be a lot harder this way. But Mama would say, that doesn't give me an excuse not to try.

She shifted the books so she could touch the stitches

of the lotus on her sleeve and smooth the fabric into place. Inhaling sharply, she went back to the lean-to's threshold and kicked the doorframe, loud enough to be heard in the schoolroom.

The talk stopped at once.

Hanna set her books down on a shelf. She took off her bonnet and hung it on a peg. The space around her suddenly felt enormous, her face and head now exposed.

She inhaled deeply and breathed out with a whoosh. Then she squared her shoulders and stepped into the schoolroom. Keeping her gaze straight ahead, she walked the few paces to her desk. Out of the corner of her eye, she saw the reactions of the other girls.

Margaret drew back a step.

Edith stayed where she was. Bess turned toward Hanna, the smallest of movements, so subtle that Hanna thought she might have imagined it.

And Dolly?

Dolly's mouth and eyes were perfect circles of astonishment. Plainly, it hadn't even occurred to her to try to disguise her surprise. *She might be more honest than the others. Or not as well brought up.*

The air was so heavy with tension that when Miss

Walters spoke, her voice seemed muffled. "Good morning, Hanna," she said. "I'm just going to ring the bell now."

"Good morning," Hanna replied. She was startled that her own voice sounded quite calm. Quickly she slid into her seat and opened her reader.

For the moment, it seemed that the girls were following Miss Walters's example—acting as if nothing was out of the ordinary. They made their way to their desks as the bell rang and the other students began entering. Hanna didn't dare steal a glance at Dolly's face.

The younger pupils moved toward the front of the room. None of them took any notice of her. But as the older boys went to their places across the center aisle, Hanna heard whispering. She kept her eyes resolutely on her book even as those whispers seemed to crawl down her spine.

"Quiet, please," Miss Walters said firmly. "Fifth Reader class, please choose a selection and use it for your grammar lesson. Parse a sentence of at least ten words on your slates. Fourth Reader class, rise and come forward."

She's not asking the Fifth Reader class to come to the front. Which spares me having to stand up there.

Miss Walters did not look in Hanna's direction, but Hanna sensed the most fragile of ties between them.

BY THE END OF THE MORNING, all but the youngest students were aware of Hanna. The room seethed with suppressed excitement and curiosity. Miss Walters called for quiet again, this time in a sharper voice, which kept students from turning around to stare.

Hanna was mired in misery. What would happen at the noon hour? Should she stay in her seat? Every student in the school would pass her desk on the way out. She could not bear the thought of their stares and whispers. But if she got up quickly and was first out the door, it would look like she was running away.

Miss Walters was hearing the youngest students recite their arithmetic lesson. When they were finished, she rose from her chair and walked around to the front of her desk.

"I have a special assignment for each one of you," she said. "LaForge is a new town, and we are all new here. Please go home for your dinners, and return prepared to tell me about where each of you have come from—where you were born and lived before you moved to LaForge. You are dismissed."

As the teacher was speaking, an idea came to Hanna. She picked up her dinner pail, which had been on the floor at her feet, and put it on her desk. Then she bowed her head, folded her hands in front of her face, and closed her eyes.

Not even the boldest student would dare bother her if she was saying grace.

Hanna raised her head and glanced around slowly. The room was almost empty. Near the front, the two homestead children were opening their dinner pails, with Miss Walters knitting at her desk just beyond. No one said anything to Hanna.

Her stomach was so tight that she had no appetite,

but she forced herself to swallow her corn cake. Having sat stiffly at her desk for the whole morning, she felt achy all over. She slid out of her seat and put her weight on her feet gingerly, testing to see if her legs would tremble. They seemed steady enough, so she stepped to the stove in the middle of the room. It was unlit, for the weather was warm these days; the water pail sat on the floor next to it, with the dipper hanging from one of the stove's handles. She ladled up some water and began to drink thirstily.

Before she had finished, a little girl came into the schoolhouse and approached the stove.

"Please, miss, would you dip for me, too?"

Startled, Hanna almost dropped the dipper. On the other side of the stove, the girl was looking at her. She couldn't have been more than about seven years old, wearing a calico dress under a pinafore made from flour sacks. Her face was pale and freckled, her reddish hair in two tight braids bound with thread. She was missing both of her front teeth, and her cheek had a smear of dirt on it.

Hanna filled the dipper again and held it out toward the girl, who took it from her carefully. She drank the full measure and handed the dipper back to Hanna.

"Thank you."

"You're welcome," Hanna said, but the words came out barely more than a whisper.

The girl frowned. "Somethin' wrong with your voice?" she asked.

Hanna felt her eyes grow hot; she blinked hard to forestall tears. It was her first conversation with another pupil: a little girl who apparently thought the only thing wrong or odd about Hanna was her voice.

She cleared her throat. "No, I'm fine," she said, louder this time. "There's some dirt on your face. May I?" She pulled her handkerchief from her pocket and wetted it. The girl took a step closer so Hanna could wipe her cheek.

Hanna smiled, and the girl smiled back.

Once all the students were settled again, three desks remained empty; the pupils who sat in them had not returned after their dinners. Miss Walters rapped on her desk with the pointer. She stood and walked to one side of the room. The blackboard wrapped around three walls; she took up a piece of chalk and stood near the board on the left wall.

"First Reader class, please come forward."

The First Reader class was two children: the little girl whose face Hanna had wiped, and a boy with a prominent cowlick.

"Pearl, where were you born?"

"I was born in Minnesota, miss."

Miss Walters wrote *Minnesota* on the blackboard. "Did you live on a farm in Minnesota?"

"Yes, miss."

"Freddie, what about you?"

"Ohio, miss. My pa is from there. Then we lived in Illinois, where my ma is from."

The teacher wrote those two states on the board as well. Freddie's family had come to LaForge from Chicago.

Chicago! From the mild stirring in the room, Hanna could tell that the other students were as impressed as she was by the mention of that enormous city.

Miss Walters smiled. "Freddie, would you like to tell us something you remember about Chicago?"

"The rail yard," Freddie answered at once. "There was so many trains—"

"Were, Freddie. There *were* so many trains."

Freddie looked surprised. "You seen them too, miss?"

Miss Walters quickly covered her mouth with her hand to hide her amusement. "No, Freddie, I haven't. I was correcting your grammar. Thank you, Pearl and Freddie. Matthew, perhaps you will tell us a little more about Chicago when it's your turn." Miss Walters nodded at an older boy, who must have been Freddie's brother.

Each class took its turn. The Third Reader class included a girl named Sadie, who was Bess Harris's younger sister. By the time the Fourth Reader class was finished, there were seven states on the board—Wisconsin, Nebraska, Iowa, and New York had joined the list. A girl named Louisa had once visited New York City. A boy named Henry had found fossils on the shoreline of Lake Superior. And Freddie's brother, Matthew, told how they had once seen fifty trains in one day.

Gasps from around the room, and a Third Reader boy raised his hand.

"Miss, he must mean fifty *cars*, right? Fifty railroad cars, not fifty trains."

Matthew shook his head firmly. "Trains. Freddie was counting cars at first, but there were so many, it got so he couldn't count high enough, and then I said we should count *trains* instead. And it wasn't even the whole day, just the morning."

Fifty trains in a single morning! LaForge had only two trains a day, one each in the morning and afternoon, although Papa had told Hanna the railway company was supposed to be increasing the number soon.

"Fifth Reader class to the front, please," Miss Walters announced.

Hanna's pulse quickened. It did not seem possible that she could stand in front of the whole school, but staying seated would be worse: It would attract just as much attention and be disobedient as well.

The Fifth Reader class was the largest, five girls, three boys. As Hanna walked toward the front of the room, her stomach was so cold she could hardly breathe. At this moment, many of the students were getting their first really good look at her. She felt their stares, heard the rustles as they shifted in their chairs and nudged their seatmates. A fog of suspicion and hostility seemed to surround her. When she reached the space in front of the teacher's desk, she meant to stand there proudly, with her head high, but somehow she ended up staring at the floor.

Miss Walters did not waste a single moment.

"Hanna, would you tell us where you were born?"

The teacher's voice was calm and ordinary—yet it seemed to cut through that bleak dense fog.

Talk to her. To the teacher. Don't think about anyone else. That's how I can do this—with her help. Hanna lifted her chin and looked at Miss Walters's face, then answered the question as if no one else was in the room.

"California, miss."

The other pupils could no longer contain themselves or their astonishment.

"California!"

"—always wanted to go there!"

"Did she see the ocean?"

Hanna finally dared to look at the faces in front of her. Instead of the suspicion she had felt moments earlier, she saw surprise and curiosity, interest and eagerness.

Miss Walters had done that. With a single simple question.

The teacher held up her hand to dispel the clamor, then

wrote *California* on the board. "Tell us something about California, Hanna."

She was ready for this; she had thought about it while listening to the other pupils.

"There are lots of orange trees," she said. "Mostly outside the city—outside Los Angeles, in groves. But sometimes you can see them on the hillsides or by the side of the road, or even in people's yards."

Sam stepped forward from the line of students, his hand raised.

"Yes, Sam?" Miss Walters said.

He turned to address Hanna. "Did you eat oranges every day? I only had one once, for Christmas. Two years back."

This time, there was no doubt: He was looking right at her and smiling. Not a big smile, but she could see the spark in his eye.

"Me, too, miss! I had one for Christmas too!"

"I never had one! Are they good?"

"Best thing you'll ever eat! Except for maybe Christmas candy."

"—in my stocking—"

"—at a party once."

Hanna remembered the bowl Mama had kept on the kitchen window ledge, of blue and white porcelain painted with lotuses and chrysanthemums. It almost always held oranges . . .

"Yes," she said. "We had them nearly every day."

And she felt a keen pang, realizing only then how much she missed oranges. Especially their sweet, sharp scent, which filled the air whenever one was peeled.

"Thank you, Hanna," Miss Walters said.

The rest of the students had their turn. Sam was from Minnesota; it turned out that he was little Pearl's older brother. Margaret and Albert, siblings from Iowa; Edith from Illinois. Ned was from Wisconsin. And Dolly's family had come from upstate New York.

When it was Bess's turn, she said, "I was born in Wisconsin. We also lived in Kansas and Iowa—that's where Sadie was born—and like she said, we came here from Minnesota. Ma says it's because Pa has an itchy foot."

As Hanna listened to her classmates, she glanced occasionally at Miss Walters.

She made them—she made us see that we all came from somewhere else.

For the rest of the afternoon, Hanna studied her lessons

and responded when called on. She answered questions in geography and history, worked problems in long division, and began memorizing the first table of four-syllable words in the speller.

The schoolroom was quiet and orderly. There was no chatter or laughter. It was an ordinary afternoon for the students of the LaForge school, and Hanna enjoyed reading and reciting the lessons so much that she didn't want the day to end.

The warmth of her contentment continued once she was at home, through afternoon chores and supper. She was so full of the news of her day, she skated right over the fact that Papa hardly said a word.

Then they heard a knock on the door, and from the way he looked up, she knew he'd been expecting it.

Papa opened the door, with Hanna behind him.

"Evening, Edmunds."

It was Mr. Harris.

"I'll be right along," Papa said.

"We're meeting at the depot. I'll wait for you out here."

Papa closed the door and took his hat from the wall peg. Hanna noticed then that he was wearing his good white shirt, and that his hair was carefully combed. He looked back at her and shrugged.

"Harris came by the shop site this afternoon," he said. "A couple of folks have been to see him, about your being in school. So the school board called a meeting tonight."

Hanna reached for her bonnet.

"What do you think you're about? You stay right here,

young lady. Harris wants me to attend the meeting, but he and the other board members and Miss Walters are going to do the talking, and that's as it should be." He opened the door. "Don't wait up," he said over his shoulder. "I'll tell you about it in the morning."

The sun had not yet set, so Hanna could see the two men walking up the street toward the depot at the north end of town.

The depot stood next to the railroad tracks. It had windows in all four walls. If she crouched down between two of the windows, she would probably be able to hear through the chinks in the boards.

As she tied on her bonnet, she felt a twinge of regret about disobeying Papa. It was her duty and responsibility to obey him. But there were times when she simply couldn't, and over the past year or so, those times had become more frequent.

She thought it might be partly because Mama was no longer with them. Sometimes Mama had taken her side in an argument, and together they had been able to talk Papa around. Now Hanna had to stand up to Papa alone. Irritable, snappish, dour, resentful—all his bad traits had worsened after Mama died. Hanna often found it easier not to argue with him, just to do what she wanted and hope he didn't find out.

This time she planned to be back long before he was, so he would never even know she'd been gone.

She went out the back door so she could walk behind the stores and houses instead of down Main Street. The grocery was the last building before the depot. She paused for a moment in its shadow.

Then, keeping wide of the depot, Hanna walked to its far side, where she couldn't be seen from the street. Lantern light shone from the windows. She took a quick glance around, then hurried closer, bent over double, and crept to the east end of the building. The sun was almost gone now, and most of the depot stood in shadow.

She crouched with her back against the wall. Sure enough, she heard a low rumble of voices inside. She could not make out words, but it seemed that the meeting had not yet begun. The creak of the door's hinges meant that people were still arriving. Once the meeting started, they would be speaking one at a time, and she'd be able to hear more clearly. She'd have to pay close attention so she could leave before the meeting ended and get home before Papa did.

Suddenly, Hanna saw movement on her right. Someone was approaching the depot stealthily, just as she had. Heart thumping, Hanna stayed very still. *If I don't move, maybe they won't see me, whoever they are . . .*

To her complete dismay, the person headed straight in her direction. Then she heard a loud whisper.

"I knew you'd be here."

Even in the gloom, she could see his smile.

It was Sam.

"What are you doing?" she whispered back as a wave of panic rolled over her. *Why is he here? Now I'm twice as likely to get caught.*

He crouched next to her. "Same as you," he said. "I want to hear what they say."

"Are your folks here?"

"Just my pa." A pause. "My ma, she—she keeps to herself mostly. Did you really have oranges every day?"

Taken aback by the abrupt change of subject, she stared at him for a moment and found herself answering the question. "Yes. No. Not every day, but almost. Did you think I was lying?"

"No, course not."

"Then why did you ask me again?"

"Just so's I could hear you say it one more time." He shook his head, then grinned. "An orange every day—wouldn't that be something?"

Inside, Mr. Harris's voice cut through the murmurs. "Can we all come to order, please?"

Hanna put a finger to her lips and saw that Sam was making the same gesture. She realized then that she was glad not to be alone. No, that wasn't quite right, because it wouldn't feel the same with just anyone. She was glad *he* was here, and her cheeks warmed at the thought.

The noise settled. Mr. Harris went on, "I know folks here have some concerns about a new student who began attending school yesterday. You'll all be able to have your say, but I'd like to start with Miss Walters."

A quiet moment, and then Miss Walters began to speak. Her voice did not carry as well as Mr. Harris's. Slowly, cautiously, Hanna rose from her crouch so she was standing next to the window rather than hunched beneath it. Sam did the same, on the other side of the window.

"—attended school yesterday and today. I would like you to know that she is a fine student. She has comported herself perfectly and has been kind to her schoolmates as well."

Hanna frowned. *Kind? When?*

Miss Walters went on, "There has been absolutely no trouble resulting from her attendance, nor do I expect any. Indeed, I would say the opposite: that her scholarship and behavior will serve as an excellent example to the other students."

"But she doesn't belong here!"

"I don't want her in school with my children!"

"*Order!*" Mr. Harris raised his voice. "I said you'd all be given a chance to speak. I intend to run this meeting in a civilized manner, and if anyone causes trouble, why, I'll have to bring in the justice of the peace."

The crowd laughed, for Mr. Harris was himself the justice of the peace.

"Thank you, Miss Walters," he said next. "I now call on Philip Harris."

Laughter again: Mr. Harris was calling on himself.

"I've known Ben Edmunds for a good few years," he said. "First met him out in Kansas. He helped me build a house there, for me and Sarah Lynn and our children. Went without a house himself so we could get ours done first. Fetched us goods from town more than once, a thirty-mile walk each way. You couldn't ask for a better neighbor. So you've heard Miss Walters talk about his daughter, and now I've told you about Ben himself. To my mind, they're exactly the kind of folks we want here in LaForge."

"What about his wife? She's a Chinaman, that's what I heard—"

"Where is she? How come no one's met her yet?"

"Too ashamed, I'll wager. He knows she's not fit to live among decent folks."

The last voice, a man's. A man who had never known Mama. Hanna's hands curled into fists so tight that her nails cut into her palms.

She swallowed hard, then glanced at Sam. He had turned to face the wall, his ear close to the window. In the dim light from inside, she could see his lips pressed together, his brow rigid. He did not look at her.

She drew in a quick breath. Was Sam's father the one who had said that?

Everyone seemed to be talking at once, their voices agitated. The commotion went on for a few moments, until the sharp rap of wood on wood.

"*Order!*" Mr. Harris shouted. "We're going to talk about this as reasonable folks. As Christians, do you hear me? Now, Bill Baxter, you seem to want to speak, so go on ahead."

Hanna remembered that Baxter was Sam's last name. She kept very still, careful not to look in his direction.

"Harris, we're all here to build new lives for our families," said Mr. Baxter. "We've got the chance to make this town just the way we want it. And what we don't want is trouble."

At least we agree on that, Hanna thought grimly.

"I wouldn't argue with a single thing you've said." Mr. Harris's voice again. "As far as I can see, neither Edmunds nor his daughter has bothered anyone in the least. Fact is, their family has already done quite a bit of good here in LaForge. Charlie? Charlie Hart, where are you?"

"Right here, Mr. Harris."

"Charlie, where are you working these days?"

"Main Street, putting up Edmunds's new store building."

"Is he paying you fairly?"

"A good wage, and my dinner as well."

"A new building," Mr. Harris said. "You've all seen the site, across from Wilson's Hardware. It's going up right now, which means that Edmunds is a regular customer at Wilson's store and the lumberyard. And the livery. And most of the other places in town. Anybody here got objections to taking his money? I sure don't."

A few guffaws.

"And likely you've heard by now that it's going to be a shop for dress goods. I imagine that the ladies are looking forward to the grand opening."

The room had grown quiet. There was a brief rumble of voices before Mr. Harris spoke again.

"I think it's time we heard from Ben Edmunds now."

Papa.

HANNA HELD HER BREATH. She heard Papa clear his throat.

"My wife's name was May," he began. "She passed away about three years ago, when Hanna was eleven."

Hanna sensed surprise in the hush that followed. Then she heard a few murmurs of what might have been sympathy.

"May was a Christian, raised by missionaries," Papa went on. "After she died, my daughter had her lessons from a good church woman. Now she's got it in her head that she wants to graduate. I figure she needs maybe two more terms of school. Then she'll be helping me at the new shop. We aim to settle down here and run a good business." A pause. "If there's going to be any trouble, it won't be either of us starting it."

Silence.

"I'm not saying to chase them out of town." Baxter's voice again. "But there's gotta be laws about this. I know coloreds can't go to school with our kids. Indians can't either. Isn't it the same for Chinamen?"

"There's a question! What's the law, Harris?" someone else called out.

Yet another clamor began, followed by the rapping sound.

This time, Mr. Harris spoke slowly. "I have to admit, I don't know where the law stands on this," he said. "I tell you what. There's no statehouse as yet—we're governed from Washington. I'll write a few letters of inquiry, and I'll call another meeting once I hear back."

Apparently Mr. Baxter was still not satisfied. "And she'll be kept out of school until then?"

"No. She'll attend school as long as there are no problems, and it'll be up to Miss Walters to decide otherwise, same as with any other student."

"But that might be breaking the law!"

Now a voice that Hanna hadn't heard before. "We don't know that. It might just as well be breaking the law to keep her *out* of school. As a school board member, I've got to go by what I know. Last place I was on the board was Ohio, and there every child under the age of sixteen has to be in school."

"Same in New York State," someone else agreed.

"But they probably don't have Chinamen living there." Mr. Baxter again. "If they did, you know there'd be a law against it—"

"Baxter." Mr. Harris's voice was firm. "We've made our decision. You don't like it, you can write your own letters."

"I might just do that." Mr. Baxter sounded belligerent but said nothing more.

Hanna realized that the meeting was likely to end soon. She ducked down low again and began creeping away from the depot.

"Hanna!" Sam called to her in a loud whisper.

She stopped and looked back, worried that if she didn't, he'd raise his voice loud enough for someone to notice.

"I'll see you in school," he said.

She could hear the smile in his voice.

As she hurried home, she tried to recall every word of the meeting. But she soon found herself thinking about Sam instead. She couldn't help smiling, and her cheeks flushed again.

The thrill was only momentary.

Although she and Papa had never spoken of it, she had gradually come to realize what leaving California had meant for her future. In the Chinatowns of Los Angeles and San Francisco, there were so many men and so few women that she might have been able to marry a Chinese man, despite being half-white.

But the farther east they traveled, the fewer Asians they had seen, and here in the eastern half of Dakota Territory, there didn't seem to be any at all. Besides which, every territory that had become a state in recent years had made it illegal for whites and nonwhites to marry.

So Hanna was quietly making plans for a future that would see her dependent on no one except herself. Graduation. Then a shop as a seamstress, first with Papa, and someday on her own.

She shook her head as if to shed the image of Sam's friendly face. No room in those plans for daydreaming about a white boy, no matter how kind.

Once home, she hurried up the stairs and got ready for bed. Papa had installed a board wall in the attic of the rented house, dividing it into two rooms; her half was at the back of the house. She was sliding under the quilt when she heard him come in.

Moments later his tread sounded on the stairs. He climbed halfway and stopped.

"Hanna," he said, his voice low.

She clutched the edge of the quilt. She couldn't see his face, couldn't tell what his tone of voice meant.

"Yes, Papa? I—I'm not asleep yet." How ridiculous. If she was answering him, of course she wasn't asleep.

"We'll talk in the morning," he said. "But if you're going to disobey me, you'll have to learn to cover your tracks better. You left the door unlatched."

That was all. Before she could reply, he went back down the stairs.

Hanna drew in a deep breath. She smiled as she turned on her side and curled up a little.

Papa could still surprise her sometimes.

The next morning, Hanna knew what Papa would say before he said it.

"I don't know, Hanna. People are already riled—I don't like the smell of it."

She paused before she spoke. "Mr. Harris said I could

attend school until he hears back from Washington on what the law is."

No answer.

Yesterday afternoon had given her a tantalizing glimpse of school at its best. If she could have lessons like that for the rest of the term, she could graduate as Mama had wanted.

There was another reason, though—a more important one.

The world was so often unfair, and she couldn't do a single thing about most of that unfairness. But she had learned from Mama to fight it where she could, and that meant right here in LaForge.

It wasn't fair that people thought she should be kept out of school because she was half-Chinese. If she stopped going, folks like Mr. Baxter would think she had given in.

Her face must have shown what she couldn't say, for Papa sighed in irritation, then nodded. "All right," he said. "Might as well finish out the week, now that we've put Harris to all that trouble."

At school that morning, more than half a dozen seats were empty. Hanna did not know exactly who was missing, but she knew that her presence was the reason for their absence. Dolly took advantage of the absences by moving to a different seat. She did so with just enough fuss and flounce to confirm what Hanna already knew: Dolly felt that having to share a desk with Hanna was beneath her.

Miss Walters made no mention of the absent students, and the morning lessons proceeded smoothly. After arithmetic and history, Hanna used pen and ink to write a verse from a poem for the penmanship lesson. She chose "Mama's poem," which she knew by heart:

"To My Mother," by E. K. Hervey

I know thou art gone to the land of thy rest;
  Then why should my soul be so sad?
I know thou art gone where the weary are blest,
  And the mourner looks up and is glad . . .

Hanna loved practicing her penmanship. She cherished a memory from when she was a small girl in Los Angeles, of being given a brush and a little pot of ink to experiment with while Mama and a group of friends practiced Chinese brush writing. In their hands, the brushes had seemed almost alive, their movements fluid and airy and solid all at the same time. Their lettering was a song of ink that flowed from the bristles.

Hanna could not yet read, but she copied some of the shapes that the adults were making. One of Mama's friends praised her efforts. *"Already, she has a good eye."* Mama replied with obligatory modesty. *"She's so young. Who knows if it will grow with her?"* But she gave Hanna a little sideways smile that made her so proud.

Mama had gotten sick before she could teach Hanna much more about calligraphy. Writing with a pen was nothing like lettering with a brush; the pen seemed labored and scratchy by comparison. Still, perfecting her handwriting was another way that Hanna sought to keep Mama close and clear—to stop her from slipping into a hazy memory.

Hanna thought penmanship was a bit like sewing, where her hands and her mind had to be connected to each other. It was different from, say, reading, which took mostly her mind, or chores like laundry, which her hands could do almost without thought. For penmanship, she first had to think about the correct way to write a word, and then get her hand to do what her brain was thinking.

She especially liked the letters called descenders, and

always tried to make sure that their tails were in exact alignment. When she had done a good job with a page of writing, she would hold the paper at arm's length, so she could see the pen strokes without reading the contents. The slanted lines of the descenders lent a sort of visual rhythm to the page, giving it a form and feeling beyond the meaning of the words.

Hanna finished copying the poem and set the page carefully on the corner of her desk to dry. While not a perfect effort, it more than satisfied her. She wondered why she had never thought to write out that poem before.

During the noon hour, she left the room to use the privy. She lingered outside for a while, watching the older boys play a three-cornered game of catch. By the time she went back inside, several other students were already in the schoolroom.

Her penmanship paper was no longer on the corner of her desk.

HANNA IMMEDIATELY searched under and around the desk. Nothing there. She checked the floor nearby. Then she looked at the boys' half of the room. It wasn't forbidden for girls to cross the aisle, but they usually did so only if the teacher asked them to.

Sam saw her looking around and must have noticed her distressed expression. "S'matter?" he asked.

"My penmanship paper," she said. "I left it on my desk."

Sam stared for a moment. "Is that what they—" He stopped and shook his head. "I think I might know where it is." He started up the aisle toward the middle of the room.

Hanna followed and watched as he peered around the side of the stove toward the water bucket. He used the dipper to fish out a sodden piece of paper and held it up. She gasped in dismay: It was indeed her penmanship work. Water streamed from the paper—nearly every word had washed away.

Her shock lasted for only a moment.

He knew where to find it. And I would wager he knows who did it, too.

"Sam? What is the trouble here?" Miss Walters was back at her desk.

"Um, there was a piece of paper in the bucket, miss. I'll go empty it and refill it, because the water's got ink in it now." Sam picked up the bucket and quickly left to go to the well in the corner of the schoolyard.

Hanna was still standing beside the stove. "Hanna? Is this any of your concern?" Miss Walters asked.

"The paper was mine, miss."

"How did it get into the water bucket?"

"I don't know, miss."

Hanna took a breath. *I could say that I think Sam knows . . . but it's not my place.*

Slowly she closed her mouth.

"You should take more care with your possessions," Miss Walters said sharply. "Please return to your seat."

In an instant, Hanna smoothed every sign of emotion

out of her face. She walked to her desk and sat down meekly — even though she was feeling the exact opposite of meek.

She had learned at an early age to act one way while feeling another by watching Mama. Hanna had seen her mother in every kind of mood. In moments of anger or scorn or disappointment, Mama's face suddenly became a complete blank. No one else, not even Papa, could have guessed what Mama was thinking or feeling.

Except for Hanna. She and Mama had never spoken about it, but Hanna had somehow absorbed the knowledge that there were times when it was useful—*crucial*—to hide her thoughts.

Now her mind was in a jumble. She was dismayed by Miss Walters's admonition. At the same time, she was aware that it was unfair of her to expect anything different; Miss Walters had not heard her side of the story. Above all, she was alarmed . . . because of what the episode might mean about her classmates.

She did not want anyone to sense that alarm. It was a weakness that they could use against her.

Maybe it was an accident.

A bitter taste filled her mouth. She was angry at herself for thinking it, for having been put in the position of actually *hoping* someone had accidentally thrown her paper away.

She knew it was no accident because Sam had said something about "they."

And because as the other students returned, they brought that cold fog of ill will into the room again.

It took all Hanna's strength to apply herself to the afternoon grammar lesson. She and her classmates were standing at the front of the room, inverting the subjunctive in response to Miss Walters's prompts.

"If we had gone to the store, we would have seen her there."

"Had we gone to the store, we would have seen her there."

After each student had inverted three sentences, Miss Walters asked a final question.

"Who can invert the following? *If I were you, I would choose a different color.*"

Hanna lowered her gaze, not wanting the teacher to call on her. The less attention drawn to her, the better. None of the other students volunteered, and the silence lengthened into awkwardness.

"Hanna."

She looked up to see Miss Walters raising her eyebrows expectantly.

Hanna cleared her throat a little before answering. *"Were I you, I would choose a different color."*

"Well done, Hanna."

The students were stirring in surprise. Hanna cast a sidelong glance at the other girls just in time to see Dolly roll her eyes in disgust.

Edith raised her hand.

"Yes, Edith?" Miss Walters said.

"'Were I you'? Miss, that sounds so odd!" Edith exclaimed.

Miss Walters smiled. "It is rather awkward, I agree. However, I assure you that it is grammatically correct. All of you will now return to your seats and compose five sentences on your slates using the 'Were I you' construction. Then you may begin your reading."

Hanna made her way back down the aisle. Behind her, she heard Dolly whisper, "Showoff."

Would she have said that if I weren't half-Chinese?

How many times in her life had she wondered that? She always hoped that cruel remarks were misunderstandings, benign, forgotten in the next breath. Instead, they were most often birthed by thoughtlessness or ignorance at best; at worst, by venom and malice.

Why does it always bother me when people say things like that? What's the matter with me, that I must always be doubting —not just them, but myself?

She hated having such thoughts. At times they circled in her mind until she was so confused and dizzy that she would give in to tears. She held her breath, determined at all cost not to cry in school. Hastily she scrawled her five grammar sentences so she could take out her reader. Time and again, reading had saved her from her own thoughts, and she prayed it would save her now.

Sure enough, she was soon absorbed in Mr. Audubon's account of the passenger pigeon. He wrote of their vast numbers and described their flight with such vividness that she thrilled to his words.

The image of the great mass of pigeons overhead was still in her mind's eye as she slowly closed the book. A few moments passed before she was conscious of her surroundings; she heard Miss Walters calling for books and slates to be gathered up.

The school day had ended at last.

10

THE NEXT DAY, more indignities followed. Her slate pencil went missing. She opened her dinner pail to find that someone had half filled it with water, the biscuit disintegrated into slurry, the bit of salt pork sodden. A slate was passed from hand to hand whenever Miss Walters had her back turned. Hanna caught a glimpse while the Fourth Reader students in front of her were snickering over it. Someone had drawn a crude, cruel caricature of her face, bucktoothed and with slits for eyes. Above the drawing, a caption: *Dirty Chinaman!* Below it, the words *Were I you, I would not come to school!*

Her hurt was growing, and with it, her anger. She could feel the rage swelling and getting hotter inside her. She had to stop it.

They want me to lose my temper or try to get back at them somehow. Then they can say I'm a troublemaker and have me dismissed.

She would not give them that satisfaction.

For the rest of the day, she kept her head down so as not to meet anyone's eyes; attended to her studies; made sure that her face stayed blank. By the time school let out, she was exhausted.

But the day was not over yet. Hanna hurried along Second Street, as if it were possible to leave the unpleasantness behind her by getting home as quickly as she could. Approaching the alley behind the buildings on Main Street, she drew up short at the sounds of scuffling and voices.

"Quit, leave'n alone!"

"— catch you one more time —"

Sam. The second voice, that was him.

Hanna stayed where she was, hidden by the row of stables and haystacks that lined the alley. Sam emerged, dragging another boy by the collar. It was one of the Heywood brothers, either Tommy or Jimmy, who were not the same age but were both in the Fourth Reader class and looked so alike that Hanna could not yet tell them apart. What was Sam doing?

Sam gave the boy a final shove. "Tommy, you—you just get on out of here!" he shouted.

Tommy almost lost his balance, but caught himself and scrambled away. Sam hurled something after him; whatever it was hit a hitching post and shattered. Sam watched until Tommy was out of sight, then continued on his way down Second Street.

Hanna's heart was thumping hard. She stole into the street to pick up one of the shards of whatever Sam had thrown.

It was a piece of a slate. Written on it, smeared but still legible, were the words "*I you.*"

Friday. Never had Hanna so welcomed the end of the week. *Only one more day to get through.*

Miss Walters spent the afternoon assigning each pupil a speaking piece. In three weeks' time, there would be an exhibition to celebrate the last day of the term.

"Those of you in the Fifth Reader class will be allowed to choose your own piece," Miss Walters said, "with my approval. Please come to school on Monday prepared to discuss your choices. I would like each of you to make at least three selections and we will decide among them, so that we will not have pupils speaking the same piece. School is dismissed."

Hanna had never recited a piece in front of an audience. She could tell that only a few of the other students truly liked the idea, but no one was surprised. It seemed that such exhibitions were expected as part of the school routine.

Hanna was both intrigued and daunted. To stand alone before what would surely be most of the town and recite a piece of poetry or prose! What if she forgot the words? What if she slipped and stumbled while saying them? What if she simply froze and could not get a single word out?

Those thoughts occupied her as she prepared to leave for the day. She had discovered that it was best for her to be the last pupil to leave the schoolroom. Most of the students were eager to go, heading out the door the moment they were released. If she took her time tidying her desk and taking up her books, the schoolyard was usually deserted when she left, which meant that she avoided the other students.

Miss Walters always bade her a friendly goodbye. On this day, Hanna found herself looking forward to the farewell for two reasons: because it meant the end of a harrowing week, and because of its sheer banality. Miss Walters said goodbye to all her students. It didn't matter who they were or what they looked like, and that included Hanna.

To Hanna's relief, both Friday evening and Saturday were very busy, leaving little time for worry. Papa asked her to organize the shipments of goods that were stacked willy-nilly in the parlor of the rented house. She also made a quick visit to the shop site.

She hadn't yet seen it. Other than going back and forth to school, she spent her days inside the rented house. Soon she would begin to feel penned in and restless, but for now school was adventure enough. And after all those weeks in the wagon, she relished staying in one place with a solid roof overhead, a cookstove, and a soft bed at night.

The rented house was on the corner of Second Street and Main; the shop was on the east side of Main Street, down toward the livery. Hanna stood on the sidewalk in front of the lot and watched Papa hold the frame straight to the plumb line while Charlie Hart hammered away.

A stocky, sturdy man in his thirties, Mr. Hart had a claim north of town and a fiancée named Angela in Ohio. He was working to earn enough for a house to replace the sod hut he was living in now. He hoped to go back to Ohio after harvest, get married, and bring Angela out before true winter.

Ginger-haired with a beard to match, he was so fair-skinned that he was perpetually sunburned. Papa had said that he was a steady worker with expert carpentry skills. "Better than mine, truth be told," Papa admitted. Hanna was impressed, because Papa was himself a fine carpenter.

"Framing the front wall next," he said to her.

Hanna glanced up and down the street. The shop fronts were structurally identical: two windows with a door between them. She imagined customers coming into their brand-new dress shop and felt a tingle of anticipation.

"Papa, have you already bought the door?"

He shook his head. "Charlie's going to make it. Says it'll be better than a bought one. Why do you ask?"

"Hoops," she answered. "They're coming back in style, and they're too wide to go through an ordinary door. Women have to stop and tug at their skirts. It's a nuisance."

Mr. Hart had stopped hammering and was listening. "Huh. I've seen the ladies do that. Never thought about it before."

"It would be nice to have the only shop on the street where they could just sail right in," Hanna said.

Mr. Hart scratched his head under his hat. "Could do a double door," he said, "and one window instead of two, but a bigger one."

Hanna nodded. "A big window would be nice for displays," she said. *Of dresses*, she added silently.

Papa put his hands on his hips. "So the two of you have got that all decided?" he said.

Hanna held her breath as she glanced at him. Was he angry?

He tossed the plumb line to Mr. Hart as he strode past her. "Guess I better get to the lumberyard. Gonna need more wood for a double door."

Hanna spent most of Saturday sorting through the shop supplies they had brought with them from Cheyenne. The button box. Spools of thread, some reels of ribbon, hanks of embroidery floss. Papers of needles and pins, assorted fasteners, boxes of dressmaker's chalk. A few skeins of knitting wool.

One reel of plain red ribbon was almost spent. Hanna pulled off what was left. A little more than her hand's span, probably around nine inches, but both ends were some-what frayed and would have to be trimmed. Not enough for a neck ribbon. Barely enough for a decorative bow. She trimmed the ends and rolled up the short length carefully, then set it aside. She'd figure out some way to use it.

That day she also accomplished something she'd been wanting to do for a while. The braid of prairie turnip had been hanging from a nail on the kitchen wall ever since they moved into the rented house. She snipped off half a dozen bulbs and put them to soak in a bowl of water. *They'll be ready to cook on Tuesday.*

It was a small excitement, trying a food she had never eaten before. She hoped she would like it, but even if she didn't, at least it would make that meal interesting.

On Sunday she and Papa went to church services, which were held in the railway depot. They slipped inside just as the service began, and left during the last hymn. It was Hanna's first time; the previous week, Papa had gone without her. While some of the people seated at the back saw them come in, no one spoke to them. Hanna was discomfited by the stares and the nudges, but she knew it was good that she had been seen attending church. One less thing for people to hold against her.

She reminded Papa to tithe, which Mama had always insisted on out of gratitude to the missionaries who had cared for her in China.

That night Hanna slept poorly, wondering what she would face in school the next day. The sheets felt scratchy; the quilt lay askew no matter how many times she tried to straighten it. She shifted and squirmed for at least half the night.

Monday morning came too quickly.

11

HANNA'S STEPS SLOWED as she neared the school-house. She had to force her feet to continue up to the building and into the lean-to. Not until she took off her bonnet did she notice the quiet.

She realized then that the schoolyard had been empty. No one was in the lean-to, and she knew before walking into the schoolroom that she would see no students there.

Miss Walters sat at her desk, writing in the ledger. As Hanna slid into her seat, she heard footsteps in the lean-to.

Sam entered, followed by Dolly, Bess, and Sadie, Bess's sister. By the time Miss Walters rapped on her desk to begin the school day, no other students had arrived.

Hanna stole a glance at Sam. He hunched over a book,

but she could tell that he wasn't reading it. He was staring at nothing, his usual cheery countenance replaced by a scowl, which made her stomach knot in foreboding.

"Good morning, students. Please take out your readers."

Miss Walters apparently intended for school to progress as usual, despite the absence of most of the students. Hanna saw Bess and Dolly exchange quizzical looks.

Then a timid knock sounded at the schoolroom door. Hanna turned and saw Pearl Baxter, Sam's little sister, standing in the doorway.

"Good morning, Miss Walters," she said, in a voice barely above a whisper.

Hanna sensed a slight movement across the aisle and looked over to see that Sam had slouched even lower in his seat. With his face all but hidden by the book, only the top of his forehead was visible.

"Come in, Pearl," Miss Walters said.

"I—no, miss," Pearl said. She took a sideways step and clutched the doorframe. "I'm just—I've come to fetch Sam home."

Miss Walters tilted her head a little and spoke gently. "I hope there's nothing wrong."

"No—no, miss. Ma said to tell you, he's needed at

home." Pearl looked as if she were about to cry. "Sam? Ma said that if I come home without you, I'll get a whipping."

Hanna clenched her jaw against the familiar twinned feelings of anger and helplessness. *Poor little girl. Her own mother, scaring her like that.*

Sam stood abruptly. "It's all right, Pearl, it's not your fault. I'm coming now." He walked to the door, then paused and glanced back at the teacher. "I'm sorry, miss."

Miss Walters cleared her throat. "Sam, please tell your parents that if it's not spring planting or fall harvest, the law requires children to attend school. So long as there's no illness or death in the family."

"Yes, miss." He shook his head, then mumbled, "They know that."

He took his sister's hand. She looked up at him, her lower lip trembling. He made a face, crossing his eyes and sticking out his tongue. To Hanna's relief, Pearl smiled.

They left, closing the door quietly. Neither of them said goodbye.

Hanna drew in a long breath, trying to relax her jaw. *I thought their aim would be to stop me. I didn't think they'd stop their own children instead.*

By being in class, she was preventing nearly all the other students from getting an education. *I can't do that. I'll have to leave school.*

So they had succeeded, those townspeople who were against her.

In the midst of her terrible disappointment, she also felt a moment of appreciation for Sam. His parents were angry that Hanna was going to school. They would have wanted him to stay home. He had disobeyed them and slipped out of his house — a brave thing to have done.

Miss Walters was sitting with her fingers interlaced beneath her chin, looking very thoughtful. Then she raised her head and looked at Hanna, Bess, and Dolly at the back of the room. "Fifth Reader class, please rise and pass to the front."

Her voice sounded perfectly normal. Hanna could only stare, frozen in surprise.

"Fifth Reader class?" Miss Walters said, a little more severely.

As Hanna jumped to her feet, she saw Bess and Dolly stand, looking every bit as puzzled as Hanna felt.

"Girls, you're here to get an education, are you not?"

"Yes, miss," Hanna said.

"Yes, miss," Bess echoed, while Dolly nodded, her eyes wide.

"And I've been hired to teach school. I will fulfill my duty by teaching any pupil in attendance!" Her voice grew louder and her cheeks flushed pink as she spoke. She sounded almost angry.

Hanna's gaze met the teacher's and held it for a moment. Miss Walters had just made her realize something important.

She has a choice. She could tell the school board not to let me attend. But she isn't doing that.

The families of the other students—they could send their children to school, or not.

They're free to choose.

So am I.

She raised her chin a little, and Miss Walters seemed to acknowledge her with the tiniest of nods.

Then Miss Walters smiled and shrugged. "But it does seem silly for you to have to sit in the back row. Why don't you come to the front desks."

So the three of them moved their books to seats in the second row, next to Sadie. Miss Walters opened her reader, and the school day began.

The morning was quite ordinary. The lessons proceeded as usual. No, better than usual. Sadie, small for her age and pale and shy, clearly relished having her big sister, Bess, seated next to her. Miss Walters was able to devote all her attention to just the two classes—Sadie in the Third Reader and the big girls in the Fifth. The room was quieter, too, because of fewer students or no boys or both.

Hanna especially enjoyed the history hour, where she and Bess took turns answering the questions Miss Walters put to them. Dolly faltered after just one question and confessed that she did not know the lesson.

At the noon hour, Bess and Sadie went home for their dinner. Dolly's family lived on a claim, too far out of town for her to go home. But she never stayed in the schoolhouse. Instead, she always walked through town, stopping to look in the shops.

"Would you like to walk with me?" Dolly asked.

She was looking at Hanna, who was so astonished that she almost glanced over her shoulder to see who Dolly might be addressing. But of course, no one else was there.

"I—I was going to go over the spelling lesson," Hanna replied.

"I've heard you spell," Dolly said, with a friendly smile. "You're the best in the class, you and Bess. You don't need to go over it. Come for a walk instead."

The unexpected invitation left Hanna flustered. "Maybe—but I don't know—I'd rather not go into town . . ."

"That's all right, then. We'll just take a turn around the schoolyard, and then you can walk me as far as Main Street."

The yard was nothing but bare prairie, with the well in the middle and the privy in one corner. It actually wasn't a yard at all, just the space between the school building and the street corner. The town most likely had plans for a path and plantings and maybe even trees next year, but for now the schoolyard, like LaForge itself, was raw and unfinished.

Hanna and Dolly strolled around the edge of the lot.

"It's so strange, isn't it?" Dolly said, with a giggle. "Just the four of us all morning."

"So . . . your parents don't mind that you're in school with me?"

"Oh, they don't know. They only come to town once or twice a month, so they haven't heard anything about you yet, and I haven't told them."

Hanna considered this. "What do you think they'll say when they find out?"

"Why, they'll make me stop coming, of course," Dolly replied.

Hanna said nothing. It was clear that Dolly had no notion that what she had just said was hurtful. Hanna was annoyed at herself for not anticipating the answer. And the hurt.

Dolly put her arm through Hanna's, which startled her so much that she instinctively pulled away.

"Oh, now," Dolly said. "I won't bite, I promise!" She giggled again.

She's not very . . . reliable. All this time she's been turning up her nose at me, and she chooses today to start being friendly? Not a coincidence. It's because most of the other students aren't here to see it.

Hanna took a little breath and relaxed her arm. Not letting down her guard — she still felt wary about Dolly. But it was nice, walking with a girl her age, even one she had to pretend to like.

"I never knew anybody Chinese before," Dolly said as they reached the far side of the yard. "It's kind of exciting."

"I guess you wouldn't," Hanna said quietly. "Dakota

Territory isn't far enough west. There are lots of Chinese, and other Asians, too, if you go farther west."

"My goodness, this is far enough west for me!" Dolly exclaimed. "I'd love to go back east. Where there are lots of real stores and amusing things to do. It's so *dull* out here —there's never anything to do but work."

She pouted for a moment, but quickly regained her cheerful mood. "Listen, I want to ask you something. I'm sure you won't mind, seeing as you already understand about there being no Chinese here. You don't mind, do you?"

"I won't know until you ask," Hanna said.

Dolly shrieked with laughter. "Well, of course you wouldn't! How silly of me—sometimes I just don't know what's going to come out of my mouth!"

Then she pulled a little closer to Hanna. "Your eyes," she said, "they're shaped so different. Is it hard for you to see?"

Hanna hadn't realized that she'd been holding her breath until that moment. She let it out slowly, a tiny bit at a time, which wasn't easy when what she really wanted to do was to heave a tremendous sigh.

A sigh of weariness.

12

SOMETIMES IT SEEMED TO HER that white people were obsessed with her eyes. She couldn't begin to count the number of times something like this had happened. Children pulling at the corners of their own eyes to mock her. Children, even adults, calling out "Slanty eyes!" "Slitty eyes!" "Chinaman eyes!"

Then there were those like Dolly, perhaps not meaning to be unkind, but still unthinking. Cruelty was painful. Thoughtlessness was merely exhausting.

Dolly apparently took Hanna's silence for shyness. "It's all right—you can tell me," she said. "I wouldn't go bearing tales, if it's something you don't want anyone else to know." She gave Hanna a reassuring pat on the arm.

If she thought it would help her get in with the other girls, she'd tell them quicker than I could snap my fingers. "You said yourself, I'm good at spelling."

Dolly frowned, clearly puzzled by the change of topic. "I did, but—"

"To get good at spelling, I study the speller."

"Yes, of course, but I still don't—oh." Dolly was quiet for a moment, then turned to stare hard at Hanna.

Hanna kept her face still. She knew that Dolly was examining her expression, trying to determine if what she had said was in any way spiteful.

"So that means . . ." Dolly spoke slowly. "That you can see perfectly well. You can see all the words in the speller."

Her mood shifted yet again, with another giggle. "Well, you have to admit it's a natural question, your eyes being shaped like that. Smaller and all."

Hanna could almost hear her patience fraying. "Actually, it's not really logical, when you think about it. Ned has big eyes, right? Bigger than Albert's. But no one would ask Albert if he sees worse than Ned."

Dolly blinked in obvious confusion. Then, "Yes, Ned's eyes are nice, aren't they? Don't you think he's the handsomest of the boys? But I think Sam would be the most fun to step out with . . ."

And with that, she was off, babbling about the boys.

Hanna allowed herself a moment of grim satisfaction. She had managed to say what she wanted to say.

They walked on toward Main Street. As they neared the corner, Hanna slowed her steps and broke into Dolly's monologue. "I think I'll go back now," she said.

"Don't you want to look in the shops with me? Sometimes there are new things after the freight train comes through."

Hanna shook her head. "No, thank you."

As she turned away, a wagon careered around the corner, so fast and wildly that both girls had to leap out of the way. It rattled and banged to a stop just beyond them.

The man who jumped down from the seat had a red face and a grizzled beard beneath a worn straw hat. He glared at Dolly. "Get in," he said, his words terse with fury.

Dolly glanced at Hanna and shrugged, but Hanna saw a look of alarm in her eyes. The man reached out, grabbed Dolly by the arm, and practically dragged her to the wagon.

"Pa, you're hurting me!" Dolly cried out.

"You think that hurts?" he shouted. "Wait until I get

you home! You're lucky I didn't find you on Main Street! You could have disgraced us in front of the whole town!"

Hanna stood paralyzed. *He thinks being seen with me is a disgrace.*

She wished she could disappear, simply vanish, like a puff of smoke. She tried to think of Mama—*what would she do? What would she say?*—but humiliation had emptied her mind.

As Dolly's father started up the horses, he leaned over the side of the wagon seat and spat. Not *at* Hanna—but unmistakably toward her. She saw the blob of spit hit the ground.

She could not turn her head away, so she closed her eyes tightly. For a long moment, she was terrified that her legs would buckle. She stiffened her knees and pressed them together so hard that the bones hurt.

Too much. She had thought she was getting through the days as she needed to, but today had been too much. First all those families keeping their children out of school. Then Dolly's brainless question about her eyes, and now this vicious contempt . . .

She forced her eyes open, unlocked her knees, and began moving. When she reached the schoolhouse, she did not remember walking there. Once in her seat, she heard Miss Walters ask, "Hanna, do you know where Dolly is?"

"Her father—I mean Mr. Swenson—fetched her home, miss," she said.

She was astonished by her own voice. It was as if someone else had spoken, as if she herself had shrunk to the size of a dried pea and another person had taken over her body, moving, speaking calmly.

The afternoon passed in a blur.

When she was finally back at the house, she hurried up the stairs to her half of the attic and threw herself down on her bed. She had thought she was going to burst into tears, and was surprised when her eyes remained dry.

She pulled the sheet over her head and curled up on her side. She didn't move until her breathing was no longer ragged.

And then Mama came to her.

"You remember what I said? About when you feel sad, miss me too much, feel angry?"

Yes, Mama. No, Mama.

She did remember. But at that moment, she didn't want to.

"You stop thinking about yourself. That's where the sadness

is, inside you. You look outside instead. At other people. You do things for other people, it fills you with good feelings, less room for the bad ones."

Hanna turned onto her back and mouthed the words into the sheet over her face. *Mama, I can't. I'm too tired.*

"Always, it starts with one thing. One small thing."

She groaned, threw off the sheet, and sat up. "One thing. That's all. Then I'm coming back to bed."

Startled, she realized that she had spoken out loud. She went around the board partition and picked up Papa's boots, his best pair, the ones he wore to church and to go calling. Downstairs in the kitchen, she donned her apron. She put a small lump of beeswax into a pan on the stove. While the wax melted, she lit the lamp and held a plate above the flame. The plate was chipped and cracked, unsuitable for the table. It was now used for collecting lampblack. She added castor oil to the melted wax, then took everything into the lean-to, where she knelt on the floor.

After dipping a rag into the pan, she smeared it with lampblack and began rubbing the boot. Polishing boots and shoes was one of her least favorite tasks. The combination of wax, oil, and lampblack made a mess. But at least the results were satisfying: The boots always looked much nicer when she was finished, almost like new.

She didn't end up going back to bed after all. Instead she took out and unfolded the brown paper she used for sketching, and began to draw.

None of her dress sketches were drawings of specific people. An oval for a head, a few quick pencil strokes for hair, no facial features. This time, though, she drew a dress on a slim, willowy body.

Dolly's.

She included every detail that she thought Dolly would want, the very latest style from back east. A polonaise: a long jacket-like bodice that flowed into an overskirt open at the front, with an underskirt of tier after tier of lace. Ruffles at the neckline. A large satin bow on the bustle.

It was a strange kind of revenge. She was drawing Dolly a dress that she would covet hungrily—and never be able to own.

As she mixed up biscuit for supper, Hanna considered whether to tell Papa about what had happened with Dolly and her father. Papa had seen such mockery and heard the insults plenty of times, aimed at Mama. Shortly before she died, Mama had spoken to Hanna a few times about being bullied and mocked. Hanna sensed that Mama was bringing up the subject because she knew she wouldn't be around much longer, and the thought had made Hanna too sad to heed Mama as she should have.

But she had a vague memory of what Mama had told her. Mama and Papa had been out for a walk in Los Angeles, a few weeks after their marriage. A man had mocked and insulted Mama, which made Papa so angry that he had throttled the man half to death. Mama had been terrified that Papa would be arrested and charged with assault.

So Hanna had perceived that whenever possible, she needed to shield Papa from knowing about such episodes. But it was complicated.

"Your Papa, he's a good man. A good heart," Mama said. *"Most white men? They think that Chinese women are only for—for fun. They would never marry a Chinese woman."*

Papa loved Hanna and Mama, but at the same time, it was hard on him knowing that most white folks disapproved of them . . . and it was never easy for anyone, including Papa, to get rid of attitudes they had grown up with.

From those conversations, Hanna understood that it was better to simply avoid the subject around Papa. Getting her into school had been a big enough hump; he didn't need other reminders of the trouble that occurred because she was half-Chinese. He might well have heard that most families were keeping their children home from school, but he hadn't said anything about it to her.

Hanna rolled out the biscuit dough. A sudden pain seared through her, like a blow to her stomach.

She knew exactly what it was. It had happened before and would doubtless happen again. It was a piece of her heart breaking, from missing Mama.

To Mama, the fact that Hanna was half-Chinese had been the most beautiful thing in the world.

13

In some ways the rest of that week was wonderful. Hanna, Bess, and Sadie were the only students at school. Miss Walters tailored the lessons to their needs. She had both of the older girls spend more time on arithmetic, and Hanna paid extra attention to history.

Besides the enjoyment of school, her work at home held a little extra interest when, on Tuesday evening, she cooked the prairie turnips. Softened after their three-day soak, they boiled up nicely. Hanna was so eager for a taste that she burned the roof of her mouth.

Papa had said that they tasted of half potato, half turnip, and she agreed. More substantial than a turnip, not as starchy as a potato. She was charmed by the addition of a new flavor to what often seemed like a never-ending, never-changing menu of cornmeal and beans.

That week, Miss Walters always found time during the school day for a reading session, which all of them enjoyed. On Wednesday, they spent an entire hour reading aloud to one another, with Bess and Hanna taking it in turns to choose pieces from the Sixth Reader.

Not the Fifth.

Hanna wondered why Miss Walters had made the switch. Near dismissal on Friday, the teacher finally spoke about it.

"Bess and Hanna, I have an idea that I'd like to put to you. Hanna, your father told me that you would need one or two more terms of school before you could graduate. In assessing your studies, I find that I disagree. I think you're very nearly ready now." She smiled.

Hanna shifted a little in her seat, unaccustomed to praise. "I—um, thank you, miss."

"Bess, in my opinion, you are in a similar position. And I know that you are hoping to become a schoolteacher yourself."

"Yes, miss," Bess replied.

Hanna was surprised. Of the oldest girls, Edith seemed to Hanna the most likely to become a teacher. Edith was friendly and vivacious and never seemed nervous when singled out to respond, while Bess often looked like Hanna felt—as if she were forcing herself to speak. Yet although Bess's voice was quiet, she always spoke clearly.

"We have an unusual opportunity here," Miss Walters said. "Mr. Harris has written to Washington to inquire about—about certain laws governing school enrollment and attendance. The families of the other students are planning to wait until he receives a response. There are only two more weeks of the term, and I doubt very much that he will hear anything before school is finished."

She folded her hands together and leaned forward to look at the girls earnestly. "With so few students, I have decided not to hold an exhibition. I have been thinking that we can end this term another way. I believe that if the two of you work hard on the lessons I set for you, you can be prepared to take the graduation examinations on the last day. Your scores will likely not be as high as they might be if you had more time. But if you perform as I expect you to, you will complete your studies, and the school board will be able to grant you diplomas."

Hanna realized at once what Miss Walters was *not* saying. If she graduated, the townspeople would send their children to school again next term—because she would no longer be there. It was a compromise, an unsatisfying one.

Rotten eggs. That's solving the problem by going around it. Not by facing it.

Bess answered first. "I'll speak to my parents, miss. For myself, I would be glad to graduate this term. If I can get a teaching certificate and teach next term, it would be a great help to my family. I think my parents will see it that way."

"Very good, Bess," Miss Walters said. She turned to Hanna.

Hanna waited a few moments and took a long breath before she felt able to speak. "I want to sew," she said. She looked up at Miss Walters. "I don't need a teaching certificate for that. I don't even need to graduate. I want to make dresses in my father's shop."

She was astonished to find herself telling Miss Walters what was essentially private business, but now that she had gotten started, she couldn't stop. "He doesn't think I can do it, but I know I can. If I could graduate, maybe it will . . . I don't know, prove to him that—that I can do what I set out for."

Miss Walters nodded thoughtfully. "Talk to your father about it," she said. "I'm sure he'll understand."

"I will, miss." Hanna wasn't as sure as Miss Walters seemed to be. "I'll have his answer—my answer—on Monday."

When Hanna arrived home that day, she found a note from Papa asking her to come straight to the shop. The building was now fully framed and sided, and work was beginning on the interior. While Papa and Charlie Hart did the heavy carpentry work, Hanna had been following behind them, scraping and sanding.

The first floor would be divided into three spaces. The front half of the building was the shop. The back half was to be partitioned to form a sizable storeroom and their kitchen-parlor, with a lean-to outside the back door. The upstairs would be two bedrooms and a small sitting area.

Papa was about to leave to meet the afternoon freight train; he was expecting a load of furniture and fitments from Chicago. The goods he ordered were shipped first to Tracy in Minnesota, then came to LaForge on the railroad line between Tracy and Pierre. Papa sent in the orders by mail, and it usually took around three weeks for the goods to arrive.

Hanna stopped him and pulled a folded piece of paper from her pocket.

"What's this?" he asked.

"The storeroom," she said. "I was thinking . . . you're going to be in the shop most of the time, and I'm the one who'll be in and out of the storeroom. I have a few ideas to make things more sensible for me to work there."

She had done a rough sketch of the space and written a list as well. It was a real room, much more than a closet. There was a countertop along two walls, with drawers, cupboards, and shelves below and above. The list contained several items, like wall hooks and baskets and pasteboard boxes for more storage.

Her sketch showed a nicely organized storeroom. But in Hanna's mind, it would eventually become something more: a workroom, where she could sew dresses.

Papa tapped on the sketch. "Cookstove here?"

"Yes." She had drawn the cookstove in the center of the partition wall. The front of the stove, with two burners and the oven, would be in the kitchen, while the rear with its warming shelf was in the workroom. "It'll warm both spaces in the winter, so there won't be any need for a heater in the storeroom. That'll save on coal."

"Good," he said. "Show this to Charlie." He handed the paper back to her and left for the depot.

Hanna wanted to do a little hop-skip of satisfaction. True enough, the back of the cookstove would heat the storeroom. What she hadn't mentioned was that it could also be used to heat a flatiron—a necessity for dressmaking.

She talked to Mr. Hart about a few more details. Could the cupboards go all the way to the ceiling? Dusting the tops of cupboards was such a bother. And could he put a foldout ironing board into the wall? And no cupboards or shelves under the countertop where it passed beneath the window. That would be like a little desk—she'd have a chair there for sitting.

And sewing, where the light's best.

It wasn't until Sunday night that the subject of school arose, and Papa was the one who brought it up. They were sitting in the kitchen after supper—there was no place to sit in the parlor anymore; it was too full of store goods. Papa was reading the newspaper while Hanna bent over her arithmetic book.

"Heard that you and the Harris girls are the only ones in school now," he said.

She looked up in surprise. She had not talked to him about Miss Walters's proposal. *As long as I'm attending school, it's all the same to him. I don't want to give him a chance to say I should stop going.*

"Yes, Papa," she replied carefully. "Miss Walters is preparing Bess and me for diploma examinations, at the end of next week."

"So if you pass, you'll be finished?"

"Yes."

Silence. She was about to return to her studies when he spoke again.

"A few people have been saying I should take you out of school," he said. "They say it's not fair, that you're keeping all the rest from attending."

She wanted to protest that it was their choice to not send their children to school. But Papa was still talking.

"The way I see it, you're not stopping anyone," he said. "Only the government or the school board can do that."

Hanna sat up a little straighter, heartened by his words. "Has the school board said anything to you?"

He shook his head. "Still, seems like Miss Walters has

found a solution. You graduate—that's what you want. And then you're out of school—that's what those other folks want. Everybody gets what they want."

She hesitated, trying to decide what to say.

No, Papa. I do want to graduate, but I also want to be able to attend school like the other students, and I want everyone else to see that it's only fair. Miss Walters's solution doesn't achieve any of that. Besides, why should people get what they want when what they want is just plain wrong?

She could have spoken those thoughts aloud. But she would have felt as if she was fighting battles everywhere, in town, in school, at home . . . She needed at least a little rest from the fighting.

"I'll do my best to pass, Papa," she said instead.

And after that? She would help Papa in the shop, just as Mama had done. Papa intended for Hanna to work in the storeroom, keeping track of orders, making lists of supplies that ran short.

Hanna had other plans.

Mama had been Papa's seamstress, first as his employee and then, after they married, as his partner. Their men's tailor shop had been patronized by all kinds of people, including both Chinese and white customers. The shop had earned an excellent reputation based on two things: Papa's service and Mama's sewing.

Mama had taught Hanna to sew when she was barely more than a toddler. First with a big, blunt tapestry needle that she pushed in and out of a piece of wire mesh. Then a slimmer needle on burlap, which had a coarse weave that helped her keep her stitches in a straight line, and finally on linen. Over the years, Hanna had learned far more than the mechanics of stitching. Fabric choice, color, design, and especially how to suit the garment to the customer . . . Spending nearly every waking moment in the shop, she had absorbed all those lessons. She aimed to honor Mama's legacy by becoming the Edmunds Dress Goods designer and seamstress, whose garments were so fine and well made that every woman in town would want one.

She would sew her way into the hearts of the women of LaForge.

Hanna spent the next two weeks alternating between studying feverishly and ordering dress goods for the shop. Papa brought her several wholesale catalogues for fabric; she paged through them much more eagerly than she did her history book.

She discussed her choices with Papa. Several types of muslin, for bed sheets, undergarments, nightclothes. A wide selection of calicos for everyday. Poplins, challises, and printed lawns for summertime visiting and church dresses. Only a handful of woolens; they would order more of those toward the end of the summer. A wine-colored watered silk, a black cashmere, a midnight blue velvet.

Papa objected to the last three.

"Never sell them out here," he said. "Those are for city folks."

"You might be right, Papa," she said. "But remember in Los Angeles—how Mama always had a bolt or two of silk on hand, in case a gentleman wanted a silk shirt? She once told me that it was important to have nice things in a shop. Even if they're not going to sell. Because they bring in customers, just to look, and then you end up making a sale."

What Mama had actually said was, "*Sometimes beautiful things aren't for buying. They're for dreaming.*" Hanna did not repeat that to Papa; he would have dismissed it as codswallop.

"Pick two, then," he said. "I'm not buying three whole bolts that might not sell."

She chose the silk and the cashmere, feeling victorious.

But he would not yield an inch on the question of the mirror.

The shop in Los Angeles had been fitted with a huge wall mirror, three feet wide and six feet tall. No other shop in Chinatown had such a magnificent mirror; it might well have been one of the biggest in the city.

The mirror was family legend; Hanna had heard the story many times. Mama had insisted on the mirror, and she'd had to fight Papa to get it. For one thing, it had been almost unthinkably expensive. For another, Papa was convinced that it would never arrive intact—that it was sure to break during the cross-country journey from back east.

Against his expectations, the mirror arrived in one piece. As soon as it was installed, the shop seemed grander, airier, more spacious. The mirror reflected daylight from the windows and lamplight in the evenings. It immediately became the shop's centerpiece. Accustomed to peering at themselves in small hand-held looking glasses, or cheap, uneven saucer-size mirrors, folks came to the shop just to see the big mirror and their own reflections, full length and in perfect clarity.

Hanna had lived her whole childhood with that

beautiful mirror. Now she knew that she had taken it for granted. As a young girl, she had loved blowing a puff of breath at the glass. The condensation obscured her reflection. Then she would watch as the moisture dried, and giggle to see her face revealed little by little.

She wanted the same kind of mirror for the new shop, but Papa barely let her finish the question.

"No," he said with a glare. "We don't need any kind of mirror, let alone one like that. We're selling dress goods, *not clothes*."

She knew from his tone of voice that it was no use arguing with him. How had Mama convinced him? Hanna would have to figure that out somehow, because she could not possibly become a dressmaker in a shop without a mirror.

On the last day of the term, she and Bess took their examinations in grammar, arithmetic, history, geography, and orthography. Miss Walters allowed them to choose the order of the tests; Hanna began with arithmetic, her least favorite, to get it out of the way. Bess did the same. They were given an hour to write down their answers for each test except arithmetic—an hour and a quarter—and history, forty-five minutes. The questions were difficult and seemed to get harder as the day went on.

Hours later, Hanna answered the final question, which required her to diagram a complex compound sentence. She was so tired that her pen wobbled as she circled the words and drew the lines.

"You may wait if you wish, girls," Miss Walters said. "I won't be long."

Miss Walters had been grading each exam as the girls took the next one. At first, Hanna had found it distracting, wondering what mistakes she had made and how Miss Walters was marking them. But the challenges of the tests had forced her to concentrate, and she had spent most of the time alone in her head.

Now she stood and walked to the door; she badly needed to stretch her legs. She stepped out into the yard. It was very warm, the sun heating the air without a breeze to freshen it, as if pressing hard toward summer. She walked toward the corner of the schoolhouse, to stand in the shadow cast by the wall.

"Was it harder than you thought it would be?"

Hanna turned in surprise. Bess was in the doorway. She came outside and joined Hanna in the shade.

"Well, I knew the arithmetic would be hard," Hanna said. "It always is, for me. As for the rest—" She looked at Bess and shrugged. "I'll start over. *All of it* was hard!"

"I thought so too. Those history questions—I didn't have enough time."

"I know! I could only write down one or two points, when there was so much more I thought I should include."

"What about geography? What did you write for the principal rivers of Europe?"

The girls chatted for a few minutes more. Then Miss Walters came to the door and called them in.

Bess smiled. "Good luck to both of us," she said.

Hanna smiled back. For a moment, it didn't seem to matter what she had scored on the tests. Because maybe she had made a friend.

14

HANNA WENT STRAIGHT to the shop, the first time she had been there in nearly two weeks.

How it had changed! Before, all she had seen were the bones of the building. Now an honest-to-goodness shop stood in front of her, and a handsome one at that.

The siding had been painted a pale sage green, with darker green trim. The double doors with their center panels and brass knobs gave the façade an elegant look. The large window to the left of the door let in plenty of light.

Hanna stepped into the spacious interior, which smelled of freshly cut wood. There were piles of curly wood shavings everywhere. She ran her hand down the counter that Mr. Hart had built along the south wall. Behind it were shelves right up to the ceiling, each shelf wide enough to hold bolts of fabric. In the corner was the door to the store-room; more shelves lined the east and north walls. A fancy coal heater stood in the other back corner, the decorative scrolls of its nickel top shiny with newness.

She followed the sound of hammering through the door behind the counter, into the storeroom. Papa was nailing lath around the window; Mr. Hart was sawing a board placed across two sawhorses. The room looked very like Hanna's sketch, with countertop along two sides.

"Hello, Papa. Hello, Mr. Hart."

They both stopped their work to greet her. She put her books down on the counter, pulled out a piece of paper, and held it up in front of her.

Mr. Hart tilted his head and began to read aloud.

"*This is to certify that Hanna May Edmunds has hereby com-pleted the regular course of instruction . . .*" He stopped and glanced from her to Papa and back again.

"Your diploma?" Papa asked.

Hanna nodded.

Charlie had gone back to reading. Now he looked up and whistled. "Listen to this. *Geography, eighty-seven, history, eighty-four, orthography, one hundred, arithmetic, seventy-seven, grammar, ninety-eight.* Those are some mighty fine marks there."

Papa walked over and took the diploma from her to read it himself. When he looked at her, she was surprised by the gentleness in his eyes. He cleared his throat. "I was thinking of your mama," he said softly. "She'd be right proud of you."

"Thank you, Papa." She could only whisper, caught between a smile on her lips and a lump in her throat.

Papa set the date for the grand opening: a week from Tuesday. "One more week of shipments, then the weekend to make sure everything's ready. Don't care to open on a Monday, so the Tuesday it is."

"Yes, Papa."

"We'll be moving in over tomorrow. I'm counting on you to get the rented place packed up . . ."

That wouldn't be too bad. Knowing that their stay in the rented house would be short, she had kept things pretty well organized for repacking. She could hardly believe that they would be living in a house of their own. Would this be the last time she would have to pack for moving?

Papa was still speaking. ". . . those parties Mama used to give?"

The mention of Mama caught her attention. "I remember them," Hanna said.

Before Mama got sick, she had hosted parties at the shop in Los Angeles two or three times a year. Those parties were among Hanna's fondest memories. She had been so young, only four or five; still, a few of the details stood out clearly.

Mama always served lemonade and another cold drink made from jujube fruits, a kind of dried Chinese date. She bought mooncakes from Chinatown's best bakery and arranged a beautiful tray of grapes and orange slices or tangerines. People ate and drank and chatted, looked at the goods, shopped, put in orders. Customers would give Hanna sweets or pennies.

Even though it was a tailor shop for men, the women were always invited. Mama and Papa had known that it was often the ladies who chose the tailor for their menfolk. The women met old friends, as well as neighbors they hadn't known before. The shop became a neighborhood hub, and people looked forward to the gatherings.

"A party would be good for the opening," Papa said, "but I won't have time. You'll have to do it."

Hanna's eyes widened. *He wants me to take charge of a party?*

It was a daunting thought. She had never given a party; in fact, she hadn't been to one since those parties of Mama's. She thought back and realized that what she mostly remembered was how exciting it had been to see a group of people in one place, enjoying themselves and each other.

A second recollection came to mind then: serving soup to the Indian women and girls . . .

You feed people. That's part of what makes a party.

There was no bakery in town, and fresh fruit would cost a fortune to have shipped in. *But I could make a cake, or some cookies.*

She looked at Papa. "I'll need lemons, for lemonade," she said.

"Cost too much," he objected.

She thought for a moment. "Ginger shrub, then." Shrub was made with powdered ginger and cider vinegar stirred into cool water with a little sugar. It was a pleasant, refreshing drink that would cost a lot less than lemonade.

"Hmm."

"And you'll need to get in white flour and white sugar."

He put up his hands. "Anything else?"

She knew he was being sarcastic, but he didn't sound angry. "Papa, the party was *your* idea. If we're not going to do it right, we oughtn't do it at all."

One of Mama's sayings.

"Write me up a list," he said. "I'll get what I can. It might not be everything you need, so you'll just have to make do."

15

THE NEXT WEEK, Hanna and Papa carried the last few boxes from the rented house into the store building. It was the two of them now; with the heavy work done, Papa no longer needed Charlie Hart's help.

The shop's second floor had been divided into two bedrooms. On the landing at the top of the stairs, there was space for two chairs, with a small round table between them. Not big enough to be called a parlor, it would still be a nice place to sit and read during spring and fall. A lamp stood on the table.

There was a bedroom on either side of the landing. Hanna's room was at the back of the house, Papa's at the front. She had already put up a curtain over Papa's window; now she did the same for hers. Her bedroom held very little — a bedstead, a shelf along one wall, hooks for hanging clothes. Mama's old plaid shawl was draped at the foot of the bed. The books Miss Lorna had given her were lined up on the shelf.

She took a long look around. Her room. Not a rented place, not the wagon, but a room in a house that they *owned*.

"Hanna!"

Papa was calling from the front of the shop. She hurried down the stairs and out the door to the board sidewalk, where he was folding the stepladder. He had just put up the shop's new sign.

It hung from an iron bar that stuck out over the door and could be read by those walking or riding down the street. On a dark green background, the white lettering was identical on both sides. It was elegant, but still easy to read.

EDMUNDS
DRESS GOODS

Hanna gasped in delight at the sight of a five-petaled lotus outlined in gilt paint.

Papa had gotten rid of so many of Mama's things when she died. He had a good excuse: They had been preparing to travel in the wagon. But since then, Hanna had missed some of those things. The blue and white bowl that had held oranges. The enameled vase adorned with birds and flowers. The carved wooden chopsticks. At times she felt as though he had done his best to erase Mama's presence from their lives.

Now she realized that she had been unfair in that thought. He was keeping Mama's lotus, putting it right out front on the sign.

The sign was bordered in gilt. It had been stenciled and painted by Mr. Clyde at the newspaper office. Papa told her that he had applied three coats of varnish to protect it from the weather.

Hanna walked backwards a few steps to view the sign from farther away. She couldn't stop smiling.

"It looks nice, Papa," she said.

He smiled back at her. "Hope the whole town thinks the same," he said.

Next they looked at the window display. The inside of the front window was covered with sheets of brown packing paper. Papa would take the paper down on the morning of the opening. Hanna was in charge of organizing the display. She had tacked swags of fabric to the ceiling of the window well, a robin's-egg blue lawn alternating with diaphanous puffs of darker blue chiffon. The effect was that of a soft, romantic sky. Beneath the swags, a simple rack made of lath and dowel rods stood in the middle of the deep sill. It had been painted sage green to match the shop's exterior.

She had chosen three bolts of fabric: the wine-colored watered silk, a cheerful calico in blue and pink and cream plaid, and a fawn-colored challis strewn with a feathery pattern. She unrolled a few yards from each bolt and draped the loose fabric over the dowels, leaving the bolts themselves out of sight behind the rack. Then she tied ribbon around the swaths of fabric, each of which looked like a gathered skirt flowing down from the "waist" created by the ribbon.

Hanna had always made it a point to examine every tailor and dressmaker's shop she came across. She had seen a rack like this one in a shop in San Francisco; Charlie Hart had made it to her design.

"I like it," Papa said.

"Thank you, Papa. But I'm thinking it's still not quite right."

"Well"—he looked again at the display—"that brown packing paper is kinda ugly."

"Papa!" she said, rolling her eyes at his teasing. He grinned, and she felt something like a warm bubble expanding in her heart. There had been so few smiles between them since Mama's death, and today they had already exchanged two.

"After dinner, I'd like to take the wagon and go out of town a ways," Hanna said. "I'm going to dig up some prairie rose bushes and put them in the window well. So that will make it look nice, and there will be refreshments. But is there—can you think of anything else we could do, to make the opening really special?"

His habitual frown returned immediately. "You always want too much," he said.

"I just think we should do something different. The shop in Los Angeles, did you and Mama ever—I mean, I remember the parties, but I don't remember much about them—"

Papa snapped his fingers. "You put me in mind of

something," he said, his eyes bright once again. "A raffle. Sometimes it takes money to make money. The prizes will cost us some. But a raffle will bring in people who might not come otherwise."

A raffle! He explained how it would work. There would be a box on the counter where people could put their visiting cards as they entered the shop. When the box was full of cards, Papa would draw one at random; the person whose name was on the card would win a prize.

"We'll have the drawing mid-morning, maybe around ten or so, before folks leave to go home for their dinners. Let's have"—he paused for a moment—"three winners, maybe? Your mama loved a raffle. She always wanted us to put up more prizes—I remember once I had to talk her down from nine."

That sounded so like Mama. "How about five?" Hanna suggested. "Three small prizes, one medium, and a grand prize."

"Five's good."

"Can I choose the prizes, Papa?"

"Suits me. Just show me what you pick out. I don't want you losing your head and giving away the whole shop."

Hanna examined the display counter, shelves, and

drawers. Then she looked through every cupboard and cabinet in the storeroom and made her choices.

A packet of a dozen needles in various sizes. A string of assorted buttons. A cheerful posy of colored ribbons. Those would be the small prizes.

The medium prize would be a length of lace, enough to make a pair of cuffs and a matching collar, which she rolled and tied with a pretty silk flower. For the grand prize, she inspected their stock of sewing baskets and picked a small one lined in bright striped calico. The underside of its lid was padded and tufted to serve as a pincushion. She filled the basket with all kinds of notions: a paper of pins, a packet of needles, several spools of thread, a pair of embroidery scissors, dressmaker's chalk, a cloth tape measure, a German-silver thimble. Then she held it up admiringly. It was something she herself would like to win.

She showed the prizes to Papa, who gave his approval.

"I've had another idea," she said, and hurried on before he could say anything. "Remember how Mama always used to invite the ladies to the shop for those parties? I think we should do the same here—I mean, the opposite. We should have something for the men."

"What are men going to want in a dress shop?"

She hadn't thought that far. "Maybe . . . a gift? For their wives—or someone else in their family?"

He waved his hand dismissively. "The only thing men will want is for their womenfolk not to spend too much money in here."

"Oh!" She clapped in delight. "Papa, that's it! We do a separate drawing for the men, and their prize is a discount! How about thirty percent less on—on whatever their wife buys at the opening?"

Papa raised his eyebrows. She could tell that he was surprised, and she detected grudging admiration in his eyes.

"Make up a nice little card as a discount token," he said. "But *twenty* percent, not thirty." He headed for the door. "I'm going to paint up a quick sign to stand on the sidewalk, announcing the raffle. That should bring folks in."

Now Hanna was even more excited about the opening.

16

WITH THEIR STEADY, dependable roan, Chester, hitched to the wagon, Hanna headed south out of town, traveling the road on which they had come into LaForge weeks earlier. During the trip from California, Papa had taught her to drive the wagon and shoot a rifle. He saw those skills as practical necessities for the long journey; she privately regarded them as two more elements in support of her future independence.

She saw patches of prairie roses by the road, but decided to drive on for a while longer. It was a beautiful afternoon, the air warm but not heavy. No one else was out driving. Chester's hooves beat a steady rhythm that she found soothing.

It feels nice, being outdoors and on my own.

The sun climbed higher in the sky; she guessed that she had been gone about an hour. To her left, the land dipped and rolled. She saw a vast expanse of pink up ahead and pulled Chester over to the side of the road.

Sweeps and swaths of roses ran low to the ground. Their petals, deep pink shading to cream, surrounded centers so sunny and golden that each blossom looked like a cheerful little face. She walked around breathing in their perfect scent—light, fresh, sweet but not cloying.

Hanna picked out half a dozen of the smaller plants, mostly in bud rather than bloom. She had brought with her a shovel, a trowel, and the big tin washtub, as well as a bucket of water. Carefully she dug up each of the bushes and moved them to the washtub. Then she put the tub into the wagon bed. Lifting shovelfuls of soil over the side of the wagon to cover the base of each bush wasn't easy. But if she had filled the tub with soil on the ground, she would probably not have been able to lift it.

Finally she gave all the plants a good watering. With the last of the water in the bucket, she rinsed the dirt from her hands. *I'll need something to put the rosebushes in. Lard cans, maybe. With fabric tied around them. And with luck all the buds will bloom just in time for the opening.*

Satisfied, she climbed back onto the wagon seat and took a last look at the prairie.

Something to the south caught her eye.

She stared hard, seeing nothing except the endless miles of rolling grasses. *Just my eyes playing tricks?*

Then she saw it again: A few people were emerging from a dip in the land, walking away from her.

Black hair. No sunbonnets.

Indians.

While she stared, a woman at the back of the group turned to glance behind her. Hanna recognized her at once: the gray-haired elder she had encountered earlier, the day before arriving in LaForge.

Their eyes met. The woman looked at Hanna for a long moment. Then she made an unmistakable gesture with her chin, both acknowledging Hanna and beckoning her.

Hanna walked briskly to catch up with the group. They had stopped on a stretch of prairie with a slight rise. They were definitely the same Sioux women she had met before.

The gray-haired elder nodded at her. The little girls giggled, and Hanna smiled at them in recognition. The baby had changed the most; although still tied to her mother's back, she—or he—was much bigger now.

They scattered along the rise, each carrying a stick. Hanna stayed with the gray-haired woman, who then spoke to her.

—To'khel yau'n he

Hanna nodded, then pointed to herself. "Hanna," she said. "My name is Hanna."

"Hanna," the woman repeated. She tapped her own chest with a flat hand and said, "Wichapiwin."

"Wichapiwin," Hanna said, dipping her head in an awkward half bow, half curtsey. She had no idea if her gesture signified respect to the Sioux, but she hoped the woman would understand her intent. If there was one thing Mama had drilled into her from the moment she was born, it was respect for older people.

Wichapiwin knelt and fingered one of the prairie plants at her feet. A little taller than ankle height, it had hairy stems that held pale purple flowers in small, inconspicuous clusters. Wichapiwin looked up to make sure that Hanna was watching.

"Timpsina," Wichapiwin said.

Understanding flashed through Hanna's mind. "Timp-sina!" she exclaimed. Prairie turnip—that was timpsina. Wichapiwin was showing her the live plant.

Wichapiwin stretched out all five fingers, then indicated the plant's leaflets, in groups of five that echoed the shape of her hand.

"Oh! That's how you know the plant, because of the five leaves?" Hanna held up her own hand.

Raising her chin, Wichapiwin pursed her lips and turned her head in the direction of the low rise that stretched toward the south. Hanna saw numerous patches of the purple-flowered plants. There was no doubt in her mind now; Wichapiwin was definitely pointing by using her lips instead of a forefinger.

Wichapiwin took a stick from the bag over her shoulder. Hanna saw that it was black and sharp at the tip, probably fire-tempered. Wichapiwin began using the stick to dig into the soil at the base of the timpsina's stem. The ground was hard and dry; it took her some time to uproot the plant.

She showed Hanna a tuber with a long taproot. Of course it looked nothing like the braided bulbs; it was covered with black dirt. Wichapiwin knocked some of the dirt loose, then twisted the tuber from its stem, leaving the tap-root attached. She rubbed away some of the soil with her fingers, revealing a dull brown husk. Finally, she peeled the husk partway, so Hanna could see the tuber's pure white interior.

"So you peel them first, and then dry them, and then use the root to braid them together," Hanna said, making gestures.

Wichapiwin spoke again and mimed eating, bringing her hand to her mouth, then motioned toward Hanna.

"Oh, yes, we did eat them," Hanna replied. "I like timp-sina." She smacked her lips noisily.

Wichapiwin smiled. She put the tuber into her sack and began to work on the next plant. Hanna wanted to help. She wondered if she should return to the wagon for the shovel and trowel, but as she watched, she realized that the pointed stick was perfectly suited to the work. Wichapiwin dug up each turnip while causing the least amount of dis-turbance to the surrounding earth.

Hanna thought again about the braid of timpsina she had received. It had held at least two dozen bulbs, and only now did she realize how much time and effort had gone into that gift.

When Wichapiwin pulled up the next tuber, Hanna held out her hand. In gestures, she offered to twist the turnip from its stem and remove some of the soil. Wichapiwin nodded. For a while they worked next to each other in companionable silence.

Hanna didn't know how much time had passed before she suddenly realized how strong the sun was on her back. *It's probably gone three o'clock, at least. I should be getting home.*

Reluctantly she brushed off her hands and stood up from her crouch.

"I have to go now," she said. "I—I'm glad we met again."

She didn't know how much English Wichapiwin could understand, but it didn't seem to matter. Wichapiwin nodded a farewell. Hanna returned to the wagon. On the way back to town, she found herself wishing that Mama could have met Wichapiwin, and tried to imagine the two women together. Chester's ears framed her view of the road ahead, which softened and blurred until she blinked her eyes clear.

HANNA DROVE THE WAGON into the alley behind the shop. Papa came out to meet her.

"What kept you?" he demanded.

"I'm sorry, Papa. I didn't mean to be so long." She climbed down from the wagon seat. "Those Indians I met, the day before we got here? I saw them again."

"The same ones?"

"Yes."

In silence, Hanna put away the tools, and Papa lifted down the washtub full of plants.

"I'll take the wagon back for you," Papa said. He shook his head. "We need to get a stable built before winter. Where did you see the Indians?"

Hanna shrugged. "Five miles out? Maybe a little farther. On the road we came in on."

"Five miles, huh? I'll lay odds they didn't have a pass."

"A pass?"

"That's what they need if they want to leave their land. They have to get special permission from the Indian agent. In Yankton."

Immediately, Hanna's mind filled with questions. Was it difficult for them to get a pass? Was the agent's permission required no matter what the circumstances? Did each of them need a pass, even the children?

Papa drove off to take Chester and the wagon back to the livery. When he returned, Hanna had decided which of her questions was the most pressing. "What happens if the Indians don't have a pass?"

He shrugged. "Don't know. That's the agent's lookout."

"They were harvesting turnips. Wild ones that don't belong to anyone. Would they have to have a pass for that?"

"If they're off their land, they need a pass—didn't you hear me say it the first time?"

She sensed his impatience. "Yes, Papa." She had more

questions, but if his mood was turning, she'd have to wait and ask them later.

As he went into the kitchen, he spoke over his shoulder. "I'll go see Harris later this afternoon, if I can spare the time."

She looked up. "Pardon me, Papa?"

"He's the one who'll get word to Yankton."

The kitchen door creaked shut behind him.

Hanna stood staring at the closed door.

Papa was going to tell Mr. Harris that those women might have been off their land without a pass. It was her fault, for telling him that she'd seen them.

She opened her mouth to protest, then snapped it shut. *I mustn't start hollering—that will only make him angry. I have to figure out what to say first.*

In the next second, she completely disregarded her own advice.

"Papa!" she cried out as she threw open the door. "Papa, do you mean to say that you're going to *report* them? To Mr. Harris?"

Her outburst startled Papa, who was in the midst of

pouring himself a cup of tea. The hot brown liquid sloshed over the edge of his tin cup, onto the tabletop and then the floor.

"What the blazes, Hanna!" he shouted, banging the tea-pot down and spilling still more tea.

"It's not fair! They were digging up turnips. They weren't doing anything wrong!"

"If they didn't have a pass, they were breaking the law, plain and simple!" His face was red now, and the anger in his voice made her flinch. To steady herself, she summoned the image of the two little Indian girls and the baby. *That first time, we stared at each other, me and one of the girls. Her eyes so dark, like Mama's, like mine . . .*

"But Papa, you're the one who told me that the land around here used to be theirs. Maybe they didn't even know they were in the wrong place."

"That's no excuse! What's got into you, Hanna—since when did you care so much about the Indians?"

It was a reasonable question. *I always cared about the unfairness. But I used to think only of how white people treated Chinese people. Now I know it's about how white people treat anybody who isn't white.*

She couldn't bring herself to say that to Papa. Her momentary silence gave them both a chance to take a breath. She spoke again, carefully.

"Papa. It might be different if—if I'd seen a big group of men riding out. But I saw women and children. There was even a baby, on his mama's back." She tried to smile winningly.

"Hmph."

Hope sparked inside her as she sensed his anger dissipating. "Please, Papa, don't report them. They're only trying to feed their families."

"You're not to tell me what to do," he retorted, but the abrasive edge in his voice was gone. "The truth is, I likely won't have time to bother with it. Now, if you'll excuse me, I've got work to do." He left through the door into the storeroom.

Not a total victory.

But not a defeat, either.

The next few days were frantically busy. Papa organized the goods in the shop, Hanna took charge of the storeroom. On Wednesday, she baked dozens of cookies. Two kinds, molasses clove and sugar vanilla—the one brown and spicy, the other light and crisp. She stored them in tins to await Tuesday's opening. She also made two strings of bells to hang on the double doors; they would jingle cheerfully to announce the arrival of customers.

The following day, as Papa handed Hanna his plate after dinner, he said, "Had some visitors today—well, not exactly visitors. They just stopped by to chat."

"Oh?" She stacked his plate on hers and rose to put them in the basin.

"Didn't stay long. Let's see, it was Miss Walters, Mrs. Tanner, and Mrs. Grantham."

Mrs. Tanner was married to the town's doctor. Mrs. Grantham owned the furniture shop with her husband.

Hanna turned in surprise. "Miss Walters was here?"

"Yes. Like I said, they didn't linger." Pause. "Miss Walters asked if we were going to be making dresses as well as selling dress goods, and the other ladies wanted to know the same."

She tried to speak nonchalantly. "What did you say to them?"

"Well, what was I supposed to say?" he demanded, but there was no real heat in his voice. "They sort of ambushed me. If they had asked me one at a time, I could have said something different. But they came to me in a group, and . . ." He spread out his hands in a gesture of helplessness.

She waited, holding her breath.

"I told them I was looking into it," he said. "So that's what I'm going to do."

Her brows drew together in puzzlement. "How?"

"I'm thinking about hiring a seamstress."

I mustn't shout at him—it will only make him angry.

But this was an important moment: If she wanted him to think of her as old enough to be the Edmunds Dress Goods seamstress, she would have to act that way.

"Papa," she said, keeping her voice as quiet and controlled as she could. "I know you don't want me to sew for the shop, but I don't know why."

He crossed his arms over his chest. "I'm your father. You do as I say, and I don't have to explain myself to you."

Breathe. "I don't mean to be impudent, but I need you to know something. Mama taught me to sew. It's what she gave me, and I'm proud of that. I think she would have wanted me to help you make the new shop a success. She would have wanted me to sew for you."

Papa scowled, and for the space of a long breath, she

thought he might either start yelling or storm out of the room. Instead, he looked at her and jerked his chin toward her chair. She put the plates in the basin and sat down again.

"People talk," he began. "When I married your mama, folks said things. About how it wasn't right, a white man marrying a Chinese woman."

She nodded. She knew about that, having seen it and heard it and sensed it as long as she could remember.

"There's more. They said I was taking advantage. Making sure I had a . . . a servant for life."

Her eyes widened. "But that's not true!" she blurted out.

Even as a child, she had understood that her parents were partners in the shop. She had often heard them discussing business. As she grew older, she realized that Mama was not only a talented seamstress, but also had an intuitive grasp of how the right clothes could bring people great satisfaction—and how the wrong ones made them unhappy. Papa consulted Mama on every order he took.

Not a servant. Not Mama. She had been his true partner.

"They were wrong, whoever said that!"

He rubbed the stubble on his chin. "That's what I think

too. But I can't change the plain facts. I'm white. She was Chinese. Folks will think what they think, and I hate to say it, but there are times when I wonder if they might have been right—if that's maybe what some small part of me was thinking, without me even really knowing it."

Hanna had never before seen that expression on Papa's face. Puzzled, uncertain, full of something like sadness or maybe longing . . . but in the next second, his brow had hardened again.

"Is that it, Papa? Because people might say the same now, maybe even worse, seeing as I'm only fourteen?"

He shrugged. "That, and a fourteen-year-old girl shouldn't have to work like a grown woman."

This is my chance.

"But Papa, I love the work. It's more like . . . like play for me."

"See, that's the problem! When folks are paying you good money, you can't act like it's play. You need to be responsible."

She would have to try another approach.

"Well, Papa, it's certainly not sensible to pay a seamstress when you've got one in the family," she said. Desperation was making her bold. "You have to admit that. So I have a business proposal for you."

He looked skeptical but said nothing, so she went on. "I want to make a sample dress to hang in the window. There's only three more days until we open, not counting Sunday, so to finish it in time, I'll need help. We'll have to hire someone—an assistant, not a seamstress. If folks put in orders because they like the look of the dress, I get to sew for the shop. If not, I'll pay you back every cent of what it costs, the fabric, the help, everything."

She had no idea where she would get the money to repay him, but she kept going.

"Mama must have known what people were thinking about you and her, but she went ahead and worked in the shop anyway. I want to do the same. Please at least let me try."

The silence that followed seemed to last forever. Papa's eyes were cast down, as if he were studying his sleeve. Finally he raised his head and looked at her.

"Who are you thinking of hiring?" he asked.

18

WHEN HANNA TOLD PAPA that she wanted to hire Bess Harris, he said that he'd seen the Harris wagon drive by earlier. The family might still be in town.

She walked up Main Street, looking at every horse and team tied to the hitching posts. In front of Bennett's grocery, she recognized the Harris horses. She stood near the wagon; it wasn't long before Bess came out with her arms full of purchases.

"Can I help?" Hanna asked.

"Thank you," Bess said as she shifted the parcels and handed her a box of salt; together, they put the groceries in the wagon.

"I came to find you," Hanna said. "I want to ask you something."

Bess looked surprised and glanced toward the door of the grocery. "Ma will be out in a minute," she said.

"I won't keep you," Hanna said. "I was just wondering . . . I need some help sewing. Do you like to sew?"

Bess shrugged. "I can't say I like it," she replied, "but Ma taught me well."

"Do you think . . . Would you like to come and sew with me? I'll pay you fifty cents a day, and your dinner. It would only be for a few days at first, but it might turn into more than that." Hanna found herself on tiptoe, tense with hoping.

"I'll be teaching school in the fall," Bess said. "I've been wanting to find a way to earn some this summer. I'd say it would suit me fine, but I have to ask my parents."

"Of course," Hanna said, her spirits lifting. "And I need help right away. Can you come tomorrow?"

Bess was about to reply when someone called to her.

"Bess? Bess, we have to be going."

Mrs. Harris was hurrying toward them. She was of average height, her brown hair strained back into a tight bun. She wore a dress of gray poplin, its plainness relieved only by a simple gold bar brooch pinned at the throat.

"Is everything in the wagon?" Mrs. Harris asked. She

did not wait for an answer. "Come along, we should be off home."

The air around Hanna chilled. She always felt this when someone deliberately avoided looking at her. Politeness dictated that Mrs. Harris should greet whomever Bess was speaking to; the only way for Mrs. Harris to avoid doing so was to pretend Hanna wasn't there.

Mrs. Harris put her hand on Bess's arm so that her back was partly turned to Hanna, creating a barrier with the angle of her shoulders and the cant of her head. Hanna was only a few steps away, but she might as well have been in another county.

Bess was now climbing into the wagon, her face hidden by the brim of her bonnet.

Mrs. Harris—she's not like her husband. Or Bess. She doesn't want anything to do with me. She'll never allow Bess to work at the shop.

Hanna had to resist the urge to cringe away from Mrs. Harris's coldness, to shrink into herself, to disappear somehow. Why did people make her feel as if she was doing something wrong when she wasn't?

Why did she let them?

Maybe I have to learn not to let them hurt me.

No. It's not my fault. It's theirs.

The Harrises' wagon was pulling away. Bess sat on the seat next to her mother. As they drove past Hanna, Bess put her hand to one side and fluttered her fingers, the smallest of movements.

She can't even say goodbye to me without having to hide it.

Hanna knew now that she was going to have to figure out how to sew faster than she had ever sewed before.

Later that afternoon, she chose the fabric for the sample dress. She knew she wanted a cotton lawn, with a fine weave that was light and airy and smooth to the touch. Lawn was ideal for the hottest days of summer, and LaForge would soon be baking under the ruthless prairie sun. After some deliberation, she settled on a pale green lawn sprigged with leaves and round berries a shade darker than the background.

Next she looked through the box of patterns that she had ordered for the shop's opening, and studied the dresses in the two most recent issues of *Godey's Lady's Book*. She finally chose one of the patterns and adapted it to include her own ideas. It would be a day dress, a fairly simple design, but the lovely lawn would make it suitable as a visiting dress as well.

The pattern called for a ruffled collar, shirred trim

on the bodice, and a four-tiered underskirt. *Three tiers will be enough. And that collar and trim—too fussy. Maybe piping instead? In a nice jade green.*

She had left the best part for last. The bodice of the dress buttoned from waist to collar. She would need twelve buttons.

She opened the enormous button box, letting her gaze rove over the rows and columns, enjoying the bounty, the colors, the shapes and sizes. Then she chose a few possibilities. Round white pearl buttons. Domed glass buttons, also white, but with an iridescent sheen. Flat circles of gold-colored metal, each etched with a daisy-like flower. She made three neat rows of buttons on the green sprigged lawn and stepped back to judge the effect.

The gold buttons didn't suit. Their color was wrong for the green of the lawn, which had more of a silvery undertone. She swept those off the fabric into her hand and put them back in the button box.

Pearl buttons were customary on a lawn dress, pretty without being the least bit garish. This sample dress had to appeal to a wide range of customers, and the pearl buttons would be the safest choice.

But Hanna wanted something just a little out of the

ordinary. The glass buttons glinted with elusive colors that changed depending on how the light touched them. They would provide the extra hint of elegance she was aiming for.

Frontier towns like LaForge, as well as their surrounding homesteads, were perpetually either dusty or muddy. Most of the women she saw followed Mama's first principle about clothing.

"Clean and neat. You don't have to be fancy. But clean and neat shows respect to other people. And respect to yourself."

Hanna was impressed by women like Miss Walters who made the added effort toward stylishness, living as they did in a place where luxuries or even niceties were months away if they could be had at all. Between observing these women and poring over the pages of *Godey's*, she had begun to form her own opinions about fashion.

The design of a dress, she thought, could emphasize either the fabric or the cut. If the fabric was beautiful or special, the cut of the dress should be simple, to allow for long uninterrupted sweeps of the material. If the style of the dress was elaborate, then the fabric should be a plain weave in a solid color, the better to show off the structural details.

This dress belonged in the first category. The sprigged lawn would be used to best advantage in a simple design, appropriate for daytime apparel. And an unfussy dress would be quicker to make. But besides that, this was a dress for the sweltering heat of summer. It should give both the wearer and those around her a sense of coolness and calm; the smooth glass buttons would add to that feeling. She could picture exactly what the dress would look like when it was finished, and she couldn't wait to see it.

Every woman in town would want one—if Hanna could sew fast enough to get it done by Tuesday's opening.

Hanna was washing the dishes after an early breakfast on Friday when she heard a knock at the lean-to door. *Whoever could be calling at this hour?*

She was astonished to see Bess Harris on the doorstep.

"Am I too early?" Bess asked.

Hanna had been standing stock-still, both the door and her mouth wide open. Now she blinked and stepped back to let Bess in. "No, no! It's just—I wasn't sure if—I mean—" She inhaled once and started over. "Please, come in."

Bess took off her sunbonnet and hung it on a peg in

the lean-to. Hanna led her through the kitchen to the workroom.

"I'm sorry I gave you a bit of a start," Bess said.

"No matter," Hanna said. "I'm glad you're here."

"Me, too," Bess said. A pause. "Ma wasn't sure about me working here, at first. But Pa and I talked her around."

Her blue eyes were wide and solemn as she went on. "Pa told her that we could use the money. Ma said that we always made do before, without me working. But that was when James was with us. He used to work odd jobs for pay, but now he's gone to Oregon."

Hanna remembered hearing about Bess's older brother.

"Ma asked Pa, how did he know it would be a nice place for me to work? Pa said that he knew your father and trusted him, and that Miss Walters had spoken well of you. And I said that I knew you from school, of course. I asked her, couldn't I try it out for just a day, and if it wasn't—if there was anything that wasn't quite right, I wouldn't go back again."

She glanced at Hanna, her expression suddenly anxious. "But I was only saying that to try to convince her. I'm sure I'll like working here."

Hanna smiled. "I hope so. Shall we make a start?"

She gave Bess a tour of the workroom, opening drawers and cabinets to show her the various supplies. "This cupboard here"—she indicated a cabinet door beneath the countertop—"this will be yours, to store your things or whatever you're working on."

Bess had brought an apron with her. While she put it on, Hanna went back to the kitchen to fetch another chair. She placed it near her own chair, by the north window.

Two chairs a comfortable distance apart. They looked as if they were already in conversation.

LENGTHS OF THE GREEN SPRIGGED lawn were unrolled on the counter. Hanna had already pinned about half the pattern pieces in place. Now she hesitated, her best pair of scissors in one hand and a paper pattern piece in the other.

She had cut out a great many garments before, of course, for herself and for Papa. But all those had been made with ordinary fabrics—muslins, denims, calicos. The lawn was the most expensive fabric she had ever worked with.

"Are you good at cutting?" she asked Bess.

"I never did before, not a dress," Bess said. "Only things like aprons. Ma cuts our dresses." She looked a little alarmed, and Hanna realized that Bess did not want to cut the fabric.

Hanna hadn't considered what it would mean to be Bess's employer. Being in the same class at school didn't necessarily mean that they were the same age; Bess might well be older than Hanna. And the white person was almost always the boss, not the other way around.

A flutter of panic rose in her throat.

I don't want her to be my employee. I want her to be my friend.

But she had to have help with the sewing, and besides, Bess was here, ready to work.

I won't make her do anything she doesn't want to do.

"How would it be if I pin the rest of the pattern, and you start basting the pieces that are already pinned? That way, there's less chance of the pattern slipping, and I'll be able to cut it without worrying."

Basting was sewing with large, simple stitches, using a contrasting color of thread that was easy to see. It was a temporary, intermediate step; all the basting threads would be removed from the final garment.

"I can baste," Bess said eagerly.

Hanna relaxed a little, feeling as though she had passed her first test as a boss.

They began pinning and basting the pattern pieces. Then Hanna cut out one of the smallest pieces, the fold-over stand collar. Basted down, the pattern piece stayed firmly in place; she was glad she had decided on that extra step. She could hear in her head another of Mama's favorite sayings: *"To save time, take time."*

Hanna had known she was lonely, but she had always thought that it was a combination of missing Mama and not having a real home. Only now did she realize how badly she had needed someone to talk to, other than Papa.

At first she and Bess talked mostly about the work. Hanna explained everything: how the dress they were making was a sample, and how it needed to be well sewn and beautiful so that people would see it and order dresses for themselves. If there were enough orders, Hanna would be able to keep Bess on for the summer.

"You'll need a dressing room," Bess said.

"I thought Papa could put up a curtain rod across that corner" — Hanna pointed — "and I'll hang some pretty fabric, and that could make a dressing room."

"What else? Oh, a mirror!" Bess exclaimed.

Hanna kept her face still, but inwardly she winced. Bess did not know, of course, about Papa's refusal to even discuss the purchase of a mirror, and Hanna had not thought of a way to change his mind.

On the wall of the upstairs landing was a round mirror the size of a saucer. Papa used it for shaving, Hanna to do her hair. Sometimes she took it down from the wall and held it at a different angle, but she could see only a small part of herself at a time. At night, with darkness beyond the windows, her image was reflected in the glass as far down as her knees, but without clarity or true color. There was no way to see what she looked like head to toe.

She didn't want to think about mirrors any longer, so she changed the subject. "Do you know what I really want? It won't be anytime soon, but someday I'd like to have a sewing machine."

Bess's face lit up with amazement. "A sewing machine? I've seen pictures in the newspaper! Do you know how to run one?"

Hanna nodded. "I do," she said. "But we haven't had a machine since we left Los Angeles. Three years now."

Mama had tried to work after she got sick, but it was impossible for her to do the fine tasks of sewing with her body jolted by coughs every few minutes. Papa hired a young white woman named Mary to help out. Mary became the shop's seamstress and worked there for more than six years, until she left to get married. When Hanna was ten years old, Mary taught her to use the sewing machine. Hanna had wanted to learn sooner, but her legs hadn't been long enough to reach the treadle.

"It seems like it would be so exciting, to sew on a machine," Bess said.

Hanna laughed. "I don't know about exciting," she said, "but it's certainly a lot faster than hand sewing. And some things like pleating or tucking are much easier on the machine. But you still have to do all the finishing work by hand. Including *buttonholes*." She spat out the last word as if it tasted bad.

"I hate buttonholes too!" Bess said. "This is probably going to sound odd, but I always hated most everything about sewing. At home, I mean. It feels different here—I guess maybe because I'm sewing for pay."

"So you like it now?" Hanna asked.

Bess laughed. "No, I wouldn't say that. But I don't mind the work the way I do at home." Pause. "And it makes me feel—I don't know, more grown-up, to be earning."

"You'll be earning better wages once you start teaching this fall."

Bess sighed. "I don't want to teach," she said. "Standing up day after day in front of a room full of strangers?" She shook her head. "Sometimes I feel so frightened I'm sure I won't be able to do it. But I'll just have to. There's no other way for me to earn good money, to help my family."

Hanna realized then how lucky she was in one sense. She loved thinking about clothes, designing dresses in her head and on paper, seeing a pattern come to life in fabric and then on a person's body. Doing work that she loved —a choice not available to many people. Maybe even most people.

"They won't be strangers for long," she said encouragingly. "You don't think of Miss Walters as a stranger anymore, do you?"

"Why, that's true," Bess said, and Hanna was glad to see her face brighten. "It's so hard to picture myself being the teacher, the way she is."

"I think you'll be a very fine teacher," Hanna said, a little shyly.

"I hope so, but—but how does anyone know they'll be good at something they haven't yet tried?"

Hanna thought for a moment. "For one thing, you're a good scholar."

"Thank you," Bess said, "but that isn't the only thing a teacher needs." She told Hanna about a teacher she'd had at a previous school—a good scholar who did not know how to handle children. It was in some ways a dreadful story of a noisy schoolroom with spitballs flying and ink spilling and almost no studying, but both girls were laughing by the time Bess finished.

"Really, it wasn't at all funny back then," Bess said, once she had caught her breath. "What if I end up in her shoes?"

"You saw what happened with her," Hanna said, "so you know what not to do. Besides, you care about doing a good job, and that's half the battle, don't you think?"

Bess smiled. "I hope you're right," she said. "I'm going to prove it. I care about this skirt seam!"

Hanna laughed. "Then I'd better get back to caring about the bodice!"

At the noon hour, Hanna dished up soup she had prepared the day before and put out a plate of biscuit. She called to Papa in the shop, but he was busy painting and said he would eat later. So she and Bess sat down in the kitchen.

Bess looked into her bowl.

"Excuse me," she said. "I don't mean to be rude, but

what's this?" She scooped something into her spoon and held it up.

"That's a dried mushroom," Hanna said. "To be honest, it doesn't taste like much. You pour hot water over them, and it makes really good stock, when you don't have meat. I put the mushrooms into the soup, but by then they've given up almost all their flavor."

She flicked a glance at Bess's face.

Hanna had grown up watching folks try Mama's Chinese cooking. She had learned that you could often tell something about a person by their reaction to unfamiliar foods. Some folks were curious and interested, eager to sample the unknown. Opposite them were those who flatly refused even the tiniest taste. Hanna often wondered about that. As babies and little children, everyone had to eat foods that they had never tried before, or else they'd have starved to death. When did they decide to stop trying things? And why?

Then there were the folks in the middle—who were hesitant to try but didn't want to be impolite. Hanna could tell from Bess's expression that she was one of that middle group, but leaning toward being interested.

Bess took a small bite of the mushroom. "You're right —it doesn't have much taste," she said, and Hanna heard the relief in her voice.

Bess ate another spoonful of the soup. "Was that turnip or potato? It tasted like both."

"Oh! That's prairie turnip. The Indians call it . . . timpsina. I think that's right. It's a Sioux word." A pause, as Hanna remembered something. "Here's a funny thing. My papa knew what it was because of *your* pa. He told me it was Mr. Harris who showed him prairie turnip, years ago in Kansas."

Bess shook her head. "We never had it at home," she said. "It's an Indian thing?"

"Well, it's a plant. I don't think plants know if they're Indian or not," Hanna said, with a smile. "But I got them from some Sioux women."

Bess was quiet for a moment, staring into her spoon at a cube of the turnip. "My ma is—she doesn't care for Indians." She did not look up. "I think maybe that's why my pa . . . why we never ate these."

Hanna recalled her encounter with Mrs. Harris. *She didn't seem to care for me, either.* But she was enjoying her time with Bess and didn't want to spoil it with unpleasant thoughts. She pointed to the braid of the remaining prairie turnips hanging on the wall.

"They braid them like we braid onions," she said. "In Chinatown in Los Angeles, you can see garlic braids in all the shops. And the Mexicans braid peppers the same way."

"Do you think people everywhere do that?" Bess asked. "Braid their vegetables, to store them?"

"Probably, don't you think? I mean, it's sort of common sense, isn't it? Saves space, keeps them dry."

By the time they finished eating, Hanna felt as if she had known Bess for years.

20

THEY HAD JUST STARTED back to work when Papa's voice sounded from the shop.

"Right this way, Mrs. Harris," he was saying.

Bess's mother? What is she doing here?

Hanna's shoulders tightened. Her mind reached for a wisp of hope: *Maybe she wasn't really ignoring me outside the grocery; she was just in a hurry to get home—*

But another part of her mind was already rebelling. *Why do I always do that? Why do I even bother to hope against what I know to be true?* Was it because she wanted to believe the best of people? Wouldn't it be easier to expect the worst, and not be left heartsick time and again? But what would that be like, to spend every hour always thinking badly about everyone around her?

She considered her choices: She could let Bess and Papa attend to Mrs. Harris. That was surely what Mrs. Harris would want—for Hanna to stay in the background, a hired girl, a servant.

Or she could do her work as the future designer and dressmaker of Edmunds Dress Goods . . .

Papa showed Bess's mother into the workroom. She was wearing a dress of brown calico trimmed modestly with narrow red braid. It was nicely made; Hanna had noticed the same about Bess's clothes. Mrs. Harris was a good seamstress, and the red trim was an unexpected touch of style.

"Good morning, Mrs. Harris," Hanna said.

Mrs. Harris nodded politely but did not return the greeting.

Bess looked up from her work with a broad smile. "Hello, Ma," she said.

"Hello, dear," Mrs. Harris said. She turned to Papa. "I hope it's all right for me to come calling before the shop is open. I thought it my responsibility as a parent to see where Bess is working."

"Of course," Papa said. "We're glad to have you here. If you'll excuse me . . ." He held up his paintbrush, nodded to Mrs. Harris, and left the room.

Hanna cleared her throat. "Bess, would you like to show your mother around a little? I'll make some tea."

"Look, Ma, isn't it a nice room for sewing?" Bess was saying as Hanna went into the kitchen.

Hanna wasn't sure why she had offered to make tea, but as she filled the kettle, she remembered yet another axiom of Mama's. *"For the person who is sour, do something sweet."* Even if she couldn't achieve the generosity of spirit practiced by Mama, she could tell herself that she was making tea as a courtesy to Bess.

These days more people were drinking coffee, but Hanna remained steadfast in her loyalty to tea, both green and black. Green tea had been Mama's favorite. As a little girl, Hanna had loved watching the tight dried leaf buds unfurl in hot water, like tiny fists opening; she loved it still. She liked black tea, too, brewed up strong and brown and gentled with sugar, sometimes with milk when there was milk to be had. In Los Angeles, Mama's Chinese friends drank only green tea, while Miss Lorna always made the other kind. Hanna had often wondered why everyone didn't drink both.

It would be black tea for Mrs. Harris, of course. After a moment's hesitation, Hanna added to the tray a plate with a few of the cookies she had baked for the opening. She carried the tray into the workroom, then invited Bess and her mother to join her.

"How nice!" Bess exclaimed. She and her mother sat in the two available chairs. Hanna poured for them, then went to fetch a third chair. *I'll not stand in a corner and wait on them as if I'm a servant. I'll sit down with them, and if she doesn't like it, she can get up and leave.*

The window on the north side of the building let in full daylight without blazing sun. The workroom was a bright and colorful place, made even more cheerful by Bess's chatter.

"Everything you need is to hand," Bess said. "You hardly have to walk more than a step or two." She took a bite of a molasses cookie.

Mrs. Harris smiled at her daughter. She sipped her tea and looked around the room. "I must say, it is all very nice," she said. "Bess, is it one of your duties to clean in here?"

Bess looked taken aback. "No, Ma," she said. "I clear up the scraps and such, but I'm being paid to sew."

Immediately, dread began growing in Hanna's heart, for she already knew what Mrs. Harris was about to say.

"I'm delighted to find the place so clean and pleasant," Mrs. Harris said.

"Thank you," Hanna said. Her hands were suddenly sweaty as thoughts raced through her head. *I should say something. Quick, say it now—don't think any longer.*

She opened her mouth and forced out the words. "You sound as if you're surprised, ma'am."

"Well, it's just that you hear things." Mrs. Harris waved her hand vaguely.

"What kinds of things?" Hanna asked. Once she had gotten started, she found it easier to keep on. *I'm going to make her say it.*

"Ma?" Bess said. She glanced first at her mother, then at Hanna, obviously anxious. Hanna felt a flicker of regret on Bess's account, but tamped it down. She was too angry now.

"I've never said anything of the sort myself," Mrs. Harris said, "but a lot of folks think that Chinamen simply don't have the same standards of cleanliness as we do. I'm pleased to see that it's not the case here."

There. She's gone and said it out loud.

Hanna had been called "dirty Chinaman" more times

than she could count. Usually the cruelty twisted her gut so hard that she could not speak. But she had finally tired of being angry at herself for that response, so she had spent a lot of time thinking what she should say instead.

And now she would say it, with her face blank and her voice as neutral as she could make it.

"Do you remember the Golden Spike?" she asked, looking directly at Mrs. Harris.

Both Mrs. Harris and Bess appeared startled by the sudden change of subject.

"Yes, of course," Mrs. Harris replied.

"I was too young, but we learned about it in school," Bess said. "The rail lines from the east and the west met in 1869, in Utah Territory."

"That's right," Hanna said. "The rail workers from the east were white. The ones from the west were Chinese."

She took a sip of her tea, trying to calm the pounding of her pulse. Over the rim of her cup, she could see that the other two were utterly mystified.

"The construction supervisor of the Central Pacific Railroad was a man named Mr. Strobridge," she continued. "He wrote a report stating that the Chinese camps were cleaner by far than the white men's camps, and that there was much less disease and sickness among the Chinese. And if you're thinking that this is a story the Chinese tell each other, I'll add that my father was one of the railroad's suppliers, and he had it from Mr. Strobridge himself."

She had been very young when Papa told her that story, perhaps six or seven years old, and she had never forgotten it.

Her voice had remained level, but she could feel that her face was hot. Bess was looking down into her lap. Mrs. Harris glanced somewhere beyond Hanna's head and shifted in her chair, clearly ill at ease.

"I'm sure I didn't mean to cause offense," she said as she stood. "I think I had best be leaving. You needn't see me out."

She left the room before Hanna could say another word.

Hanna's cheeks were still burning. She knew that she might have lost a customer; Mrs. Harris might well find her impudence cause enough to stay away. Papa would doubtless have a few words to say about that. But at the moment, Hanna was more concerned about Bess. Losing a customer was not nearly as important as losing a friend.

Bess was on her feet, having stood and watched her

mother's abrupt departure. Hanna looked at her, not sure how to begin. Should she apologize? If she did, it would be insincere: She wasn't a bit sorry for what she had said. In fact, she was proud of herself for having mustered the courage to say it.

A moment later, when Bess turned around, Hanna was surprised to see that her face was almost expressionless. "Shall I go on with the skirt tiers?" Bess asked.

Hanna blinked. That wasn't what she had expected. *Maybe she doesn't want to talk about it now. Or ever.*

"Yes, that would be fine. Unless you'd rather work on something else."

Bess shook her head. She sat down, bent over her needle, and began working assiduously.

Hanna took up her own needle again. Was it better to pretend nothing had happened, and just get on with the work?

An awful lot of people dealt with difficulties that way. Hanna was as loath as anyone to talk about disagreeable subjects, but she hated the thought of them lurking, waiting for the moment when they could rear up again.

21

THE AWKWARDNESS DISSIPATED when the girls discovered that in addition to their shared dislike of sewing buttonholes, they also both hated putting in whalebone stays. Together, they giggled their way to a solution: When it came time to put in the stays, they would take turns so neither one would have to do all of them.

"And the same with buttonholes," Bess proposed.

"A blood vow," Hanna replied. "Which of your fingers has the most pinpricks?" They held up their fingers and pressed them together.

At the end of the day, Hanna was more than satisfied with their progress. It now seemed entirely possible that, with both of them working on it, the dress could be finished in two more days.

As Bess rolled up her apron, she said, "I almost forgot. Would you walk with me to the church site? My pa is working there this week, and he asked me to tell you that he'd like a word with you."

"Of course," Hanna said. She wondered why Mr. Harris wanted to speak to her, and asked Bess if she knew.

"No, I don't," Bess said. "But he didn't seem upset at all, if that's what you're thinking."

Hanna didn't actually know what she was thinking, so puzzled was she by the request.

The church was being built on Second Street, two blocks beyond the schoolhouse. Walking with Bess past the school in the hot sunshine, Hanna was surprised by how small the schoolhouse looked. She had been a student there only a week earlier, but it felt like years ago.

When they reached the building site, Mr. Harris was up a ladder, nailing rafters. He spotted the girls and waved.

Charlie Hart was there too, framing a window. "Hullo, graduates!" he called out.

Hanna and Bess smiled—at him, and at each other. They stood waiting in the narrow stripes of shade formed by the wall studding. A few moments later, Mr. Harris climbed down the ladder and took off his apron. After a long drink of water from a jug half buried in the grass, he wet his kerchief and wiped his face and hands.

"All right," he said. "I think I'm just about presentable now, and if I'm not, you'll have to pretend and pardon. Bess, would you fetch that jug and my apron to the wagon? I need a minute with your friend here."

"Yes, Pa," Bess replied as Hanna's heart did a one-step jig of happiness. *Your friend*, he had said.

Mr. Harris walked with Hanna several paces away from the skeleton church. "Don't worry, Hanna—you're not in any kind of trouble," he began.

She was relieved. She couldn't think of anything she had done wrong, but there was something about being around the law that made a person feel guilty.

"I just need to ask you a few questions about what happened on Monday."

Monday?

Mr. Harris continued, "Your father told me that you'd seen some Indians outside their lands."

This was about Wichapiwin! How could she have forgotten?

Papa told him—even after I begged him not to. Papa, how could you?

I could lie. I could say I never saw them.

He's the law. I have to tell him the truth.

But what if the laws are unfair? Didn't the colonists disobey King George's laws because they were unfair?

Hanna almost missed what Mr. Harris said next. ". . . what you saw, and we'll go from there."

She swallowed hard, and her answer was a long time in coming. "I'd rather not say."

She saw his blue eyes widen in surprise. "Well, now. Can't say as I expected that."

He didn't sound angry, just puzzled, which gave her the courage to speak further. "Mr. Harris? I—I wouldn't lie to you. But do I—do I have to tell you what I saw?"

"Yes, you do," he said, his voice gentle but his words firm. "There's no courthouse here, but I'm the law, and everyone has to answer to the law." A pause. "If you don't, that's called contempt, and it's within my rights to arrest anyone for contempt."

Hanna almost choked on her next breath. It hadn't occurred to her that she could be *arrested* if she didn't tell him what she had seen.

"I'm the law here," Mr. Harris repeated slowly. "There's times when the law isn't a cut-and-dried thing, and it has to be interpreted. In those cases, you have to trust the man serving the law." He looked right into her eyes.

Papa had said that Mr. Harris was a fair man. He had allowed Hanna to attend school, ruling in her favor against all those parents. But she did not know how he felt about Indians. No, that wasn't entirely true: The fact that he was a white homesteader on the frontier was in itself a statement against Indians.

But I'm no different. Papa and me, we're right here in LaForge, same as Mr. Harris. This was Indian land until a few years ago—no. It still is Indian land. Stolen by white people. You steal something, that doesn't make it yours.

And if Wichapiwin hadn't had a pass, Hanna didn't see where there was any room for "interpretation."

She could tell him what she had seen, and risk the arrest of Wichapiwin and the others. Or she could refuse to answer, and risk arrest herself.

Her heart weighed down by the misery of her cowardice, she whimpered inside her head: *I'm sorry, Wichapiwin, sorry sorry sorry . . .*

"It was a group of Indian women," she said, her voice trembling.

"Just women?"

"Women and children. Two little girls and a babe in arms."

"What were they doing?"

"Digging for turnips." In her mind's eye, she saw images of Wichapiwin: eating soup, proffering the braid of timp-sina, pulling a tuber out of the ground . . . Wichapiwin, a woman who might almost be a sort of friend now. Some-how, Hanna had to get Mr. Harris to understand that. But she would have to be careful not to give him too many details about Wichapiwin, which might put her in danger of arrest.

"Did you know that the Sioux word for prairie turnip is timpsina?" Hanna lifted her chin and steadied her voice. "They taught me that. And gave me some, and told me how to cook it. So I made soup and put in some timpsina, and Bess—she ate it and she liked it—" She stopped, aware that she was starting to babble.

"Soup, huh." Mr. Harris hesitated before asking his next question. "I don't suppose you saw any weapons."

"Not weapons," she said, "wooden sticks. For digging up the turnips."

He looked thoughtful then, and was silent for several

moments. Hanna stayed quiet too, sensing that he was now making up his mind.

"That pass system," he said at last. "As far as I know, its intent is to keep Indians from congregating for the purposes of war or raiding. In my judgment, a group of women and girls harvesting prairie turnip doesn't constitute a threat to LaForge. I don't see any need to send a report to Yankton."

"Thank you, sir."

Hanna exhaled, only then aware that she had been holding her breath.

THE MATTER WOULD SEEM to be finished with no harm done, but Hanna was still furious. Granted, Papa had never said that he wouldn't tell Mr. Harris. But she was angry about more than the fact that he had disregarded her plea. Hanna decided that she had to speak up—even if he wouldn't listen.

She waited until he had nearly finished supper.

"I talked to Mr. Harris today," she said, "at the church site."

"I know," he said. "He told me that he would need to speak to you, seeing as you were the one who met those Indians."

"I asked you not to tell him."

His forehead creased and reddened. "You think you know better than I do? You were asking me to break the law."

She was ready for him, determined to make up for her cowardice with Mr. Harris. "Papa, do you consider Miss Lorna a good Christian?"

"What in tarnation—what are you talking about?"

"I'm talking about when you and Mama got married."

She had first heard the story when she was about nine years old. Back then, they had spent most evenings gathered around Mama's bed: Mama, well wrapped in the plaid shawl no matter what the season, Hanna on one side in the rocking chair, Papa in the armchair on the other. Hanna had asked Mama how she and Papa got married.

Mama started to speak but lost her breath. She nodded at Papa to take over.

"I went and spoke to Miss Lorna," he said. "She was as close to family as your mama had. And by then I'd been taking supper at her place for more than a year, so she was almost like family to me, too. I asked her if she thought it would be all right for me to marry your mama."

"What did she say?" Hanna asked.

"She said no. Absolutely not. She said, 'Mr. Edmunds, you know it's against the law.'"

Hanna's mouth fell open in dismay. "Against the law?"

"Yes. Illegal, for a white person to marry someone Chinese."

Hanna bit her lip, chilled by a nameless fear. She didn't yet understand the depths of dread possible when unfairness was sanctioned by the law.

Mama reached out from the bed to touch her arm. Hanna saw that Mama's eyes were bright; she was telling Hanna without words not to worry, that this was not a sad story. At once Hanna felt better. "You knew that already, didn't you, Papa?"

A nod. "I did."

"So why did you ask her?"

"Because I was really asking something else. Miss Lorna is a smart woman, and I was pretty sure she would understand. She said, 'Mr. Edmunds, here in the great state of California, we have *laws*, unlike in places like—like *Arizona Territory*.' She answered what was in my head, not what I'd said out loud."

Hanna stared at him, then at Mama. "You mean—she was telling you to go to Arizona?"

"Yes. She was giving us her blessing, even though she knew it was against the law. So we went to Arizona Territory. It took a little doing, but finally we found the right person to perform the ceremony."

"What kind of person?"

"A justice of the peace."

It sounded nice, the words "justice" and "peace" together like that. "A justice of the peace married you," she repeated.

Papa rolled his eyes. "No sirree. I never married anyone but your mama."

"Papa!" She couldn't help laughing. And while it was too hard for Mama to laugh, her smile at that moment lit up every corner of Hanna's world.

Hanna was certain that Papa knew what she was referring to—at least the part about Miss Lorna. "You didn't break the law, but you sure went a long way to get round it," she said. "Yourself and Mama both."

"Don't you speak against your mama."

Hanna controlled the impulse to roll her eyes at how

badly he was missing her point. "Papa, I'm not. How could I be? If you and Mama hadn't done what you did, I wouldn't have been born. The both of you, and Miss Lorna, too—you knew that the law was wrong, and you did what you had to do."

"That was different."

"How?"

"The law should stay out of a man's personal business. As long as I wasn't forcing your mama to marry me, it oughtn't to be anyone's business but hers and mine. And our families'."

Bringing up her parents' marriage hadn't swayed Papa as Hanna had thought it would, and she couldn't think of another way to convince him. "It's like you're saying that things are only unfair when they happen to *you*."

And that succeeded in making him angry. "I've had enough of your impudence," he snapped, and pushed his chair away from the table. "Tell me this: What's Harris going to do?"

She lowered her gaze. "He said that Wichapiwin and her friends aren't a threat to LaForge. He's not going to report them to Yankton."

"Sakes alive, Hanna! That's what you wanted, isn't it?

So why in blazes are you pestering me over this?" He stood and stomped from the room.

Hanna slumped back in her chair. The conversation had lasted only a minute or two, but it had exhausted her, and she hadn't budged Papa one inch.

As if tainted by that difficult conversation, everything seemed to go wrong with the next day's sewing work.

Hanna had decided at the outset to make the dress in her own size. If no orders came in, at least she would have a new dress to wear. She had been meticulous about measuring herself and adjusting the pattern accordingly. Bess finished basting the bodice, and Hanna tried it on.

It was far too tight.

"Rotten eggs!" Hanna cursed, half under her breath. "Rotten, smelly, putrid, *stinking* eggs!"

Bess looked startled. "Pardon?"

"Oh. I'm sorry. It's something my mama used to say. Her favorite curse—in English it means 'rotten egg.' I— well, I add more words sometimes."

Bess's eyes took on a bit of a sparkle. "So you can curse without people knowing you're cursing," she said. "I'm going to try that at home."

Hanna had to laugh, but then she sobered and shook her head. "There isn't enough seam allowance to fix this," she said. She would have to cut two new pieces of lawn for the front bodice and sew them again. "What did I do wrong?" she groaned.

Once she had taken the bodice apart, she and Bess discovered the mistake: Hanna had forgotten to account for eliminating the shirring of the original pattern. The shirred trim was much wider than the piping she was using in its place. It was a stupid mistake, a beginner's mistake, and she was no beginner, which only made her angrier at herself.

"No use crying over spilled milk," Bess said. "That's what my ma says, anyway. I'm going to start hemming the skirt. You go ahead and take care of the bodice and don't worry about anything else. It'll go faster this time because you've already done it once."

Hanna cast her a quick, grateful look.

23

BESS WAS RIGHT; by mid-afternoon, Hanna had replaced the front bodice, which now fit perfectly. Bess went out back to use the privy; when she returned, she said, "My, those roses are lovely. I didn't know you could grow them like that."

"Goodness!" Hanna jumped to her feet. "I forgot about them. Mrs. Blake at the hotel said I could have some lard cans. I'd better go and fetch them now." Besides the fact that the prairie rose bushes had to be transplanted for the opening, it was a Saturday, bath night; the washtub would need to be emptied and cleaned.

"Shall I come—will you need help?"

"No, no, I'd much rather you stay here and keep hemming. I won't be long at all."

Hanna hurried up the street to its north end and crossed to the other side. The hotel's owner, Mrs. Blake, directed her to the kitchen, where she collected the cans from Ellie, the hired girl. Ellie was a few years older than Hanna. Her family lived on a homestead several miles out of town; she boarded at the hotel and worked long hours cooking and cleaning for the hotel guests.

"I'd like to come to the opening, but I wouldn't be able to buy anything," Ellie said wistfully.

"Of course you must come," Hanna said. "You can look all you want, and we'll be serving refreshments. And there will be a raffle."

As Hanna left the hotel, the screen door of the next building banged open, and two men lurched out of the saloon. Both were obviously drunk. Hanna recognized one of them, to her dismay: It was Dolly's father, Mr. Swenson. She felt a stroke of sympathy for Dolly.

At his side was a man Hanna did not know. He had a broad florid face and was dressed like a homesteader in boots, trousers, a dirty plaid shirt. He held a bottle of liquor in one hand.

The stranger caught sight of Hanna. "Well, looka here," he said. "It's a li'l Injun girl."

Swenson looked at Hanna. "It's not," he said, his voice slow and heavy with drink. "Not an Injun. That there is a Chinaman. Hello, Chinaman girl."

"A Chinaman girl *here?* My, my." The other man stared at Hanna with red-rimmed eyes. "You know what they say about Chinese girls, Swenson?"

His leer was repulsive.

"I surely do, Conners," Swenson replied. He laughed heartily, stumbled, and had to grab hold of his friend to keep his balance. Then he snatched the bottle and swigged.

Quick, while they're distracted . . .

Hanna tried to edge past the two men. Swenson abruptly lowered the bottle from his mouth and stepped in front of her, blocking her way.

"Where are you going in such a hurry, Chinaman girl? I said hello. You got enough manners to say hello back?" His voice now held a note of threat.

Hanna wanted to breathe deeply, but her lungs were rigid. She could almost taste the evil in the air. Her thoughts fragmented in panic. People, not far away—just there, across the street—why did no one notice what was happening?

Both men advanced toward her; the wall of the saloon

was at her back. Surely they wouldn't do her harm here on the street, in full daylight? But if they dragged her into the alley behind the buildings . . .

She saw their faces animated by her fear, as if they were feeding on it.

"Aw, look. You done skeered her," Conners said.

"Nah, she's not scared of me—we've met before," Swenson replied. "It's *you* she's scared of. Come here, girly, nobody's gonna hurt you. S'long as you don't put up a fight." He guffawed, then placed a hand on her shoulder near her neck.

She jerked as if his touch burned her. He pulled her toward him, tightening his grip until she could feel his nails clawing into her skin. Everything went blurry. She stiffened her whole body, determined not to faint.

When her vision cleared a second later, she found herself staring at Swenson's collar, which was so worn that its edges had frayed. And the top button was missing.

Mama always said that a shirt missing a button is as bad as a clock without one of its hands.

"I CAN FIX THAT," she said loudly.

Both men blinked in astonishment, although neither

could possibly have been more surprised than Hanna herself.

"You're missing a button," she went on hurriedly. "If you'll give me your shirt, I'll take it to our shop and sew on a button—it won't take me but a minute."

As Swenson looked down at his shirtfront, she felt his hand loosen. His expression was so befuddled that she might have laughed if she hadn't been desperate to get away. She spun on her heel and took off toward the hotel.

"*Hey!*" Conners shouted. She heard the thump of boots on the board sidewalk behind her. Up ahead, she could see the door of the hotel—she was almost there, just a little farther—

The door opened, and Mrs. Blake stepped outside. Hanna had to veer sharply to avoid running into her. Conners and Swenson, too drunk to react quickly, bumped into each other and somehow ended up sprawled on the sidewalk.

"MR. SWENSON!" Mrs. Blake thundered. "I'll not warn you again! You stay *away* from my hotel, you and your no-good, drink-sodden, feckless friends! This establishment is for *nice people!* I'll call the law on you, I will!"

A few folks came out of the hotel to witness the commotion; another few on the street stopped to stare. Mrs. Blake turned to Hanna. She was a solidly built woman with brown hair piled high on her head, and severe eyebrows that looked very dark against her pale skin. Especially when she was scowling.

"Was it you who caused this ruckus?" she demanded.

So unfair! Hanna felt her eyes instantly grow warm with tears. She blinked rapidly, then opened her mouth to protest. But she was too shaken to defend herself.

"No, ma'am," she said. "I was—I'll be leaving now." She was startled to realize that she was still clutching the stack of lard cans.

Trembling, she decided to go straight across Main Street; she would not walk past the saloon again. In front of the hotel a sizable group of men and boys were hooting and jeering, pointing at Swenson and Conners, still sprawled on the sidewalk.

"Make yourselves at home down there, boys!"

"Can't hold your drink, Swenson?"

"Sweeping the sidewalk with yer face—you missed a spot, ha!"

Quickly she crossed the street and ducked behind the

wagons and horses tied to their hitching posts. When she looked again, the two men were on their feet, trying to jostle their way out of the crowd while shouting at each other.

"—not my fault, you blithering idiot! You're drunker than I am!"

"—that blasted Chinaman girl—"

Then the two men turned into the alley. To Hanna's relief, they were soon out of sight.

Hanna hurried around to the back of the shop; she did not want to have to talk to Papa. She dropped the lard cans outside the lean-to, then went inside to fetch the trowel.

The prairie roses were doing well in the washtub. All six bushes had survived being transplanted. Hanna went down on her knees and started scooping soil out of the washtub, transferring it to one of the lard cans. She dug faster and faster as tears began rolling down her cheeks. Soon she was just stabbing the trowel into the dirt again and again, weeping, sobbing, with enough mind left to pray that Papa would not come out the back door.

Nothing she had experienced before had prepared her for this terror. Despite all the pain of being mocked and bullied in the past, she knew now that her body had always been safe. Swenson putting his hands on her had made her feel so vulnerable, as if she would never in her life be able to find strength again.

When the door opened a few minutes later, it was Bess, not Papa.

"I thought I heard—Hanna! Oh my stars, what's the matter—what happened?"

Bess knelt beside her. She put her hand on Hanna's arm, then gently took the trowel away. Hanna covered her face with her hands to smother her sobs. She sensed Bess leaving her side and returning a few moments later; by that time, Hanna had managed to stop crying.

"Here," Bess said, her voice quiet and steady. She gave Hanna a damp cloth. Hanna wiped her face, then pressed the cloth to her eyes for a long moment, its coolness soothing. She took a drink of water from the tin cup Bess handed her, and finally felt her heartbeat slowing.

"Do you want me to fetch your father?" Bess asked.

Hanna looked up, wild-eyed. "No! No!"

"Shhh. All right, don't worry yourself. But we need to get you upstairs to change your dress." Bess nodded toward Hanna's right shoulder. Hanna looked down to see that her dress was torn along the seam.

She stood slowly. Bess followed her through the kitchen and up the stairs to her room. As Bess undid the buttons at the back of her dress, Hanna began weeping again. The last person to help her undress had been Mama, during her illness, when Hanna was about seven years old.

"You're hurt," Bess said. Her voice was still quiet, but now it was tight with anger.

Livid finger marks and an ugly scrape marred the skin on Hanna's shoulder. Bess dabbed at the scrape with the damp rag. Hanna shuddered and cringed at the memory of Swenson's touch.

"Who did this?" Bess asked.

"Mr. Swenson," Hanna whispered. "He was with someone I didn't know. Collins, maybe. No, Conners."

"You need to tell my pa."

"No," Hanna said again. "They'll say it was my fault."

"How could it have been your fault? You're the one who's hurt. And a girl, against two grown men—"

Hanna interrupted her. "A *half-Chinese* girl," she said. "Against two white men. Everyone will side with them, not me."

She thought of the court trials that had followed the terrible Los Angeles riots. The evidence against the white men who had lynched as many as twenty Chinese people was overwhelming. Yet every one of the murderers had been released on appeal—not because they were innocent, but because the all-white juries and judges would not punish white men for killing Chinese.

"My pa will believe you," Bess said stoutly.

Hanna was so weary that she didn't think her bones would hold her up much longer. "You and your pa," she said, her head drooping. "You might be the only ones."

HANNA SOMEHOW MANAGED to get through the rest of the afternoon without encountering Papa. Bess fairly flew about the place. She moved the prairie roses from the washtub to the lard cans, emptied out the tub and cleaned it, did more hemming work. Hanna was supposed to be edging one of the dress's sleeves with piping, but she was so distracted that she kept having to undo stitches. She hardly even noticed Bess's departure at day's end.

She put out some supper for Papa, then called to him that she was going to have her bath and go to bed. He was still busy organizing the shop for the opening and worked late into the evening.

Her night was filled with terrors. In the worst of her dreams, a giant-size Swenson grabbed her shoulder with his gargantuan paw and dragged her toward him. She could not get away no matter how much she fought, but she tried so hard that she woke herself, flailing, gasping, sweating.

The next morning she did not get up as usual. She told Papa that she wasn't feeling well, and he went to church without her.

She forced herself to rise and dress before his return; perhaps if she fixed a good dinner, he would not notice anything amiss. She felt sore all over, moving woodenly about as she made fried potatoes and fried onions to go with the salt pork. The meal was ready by the time she heard the front door open and shut.

"Hanna!"

She stiffened at the sound of his voice, loud, angry. A moment later he strode into the kitchen. "What the blazes happened?"

"What do you mean, Papa?" She was desperate to deflect his question. She was terrified that if she told him the truth, he would try to even things with Swenson, and who knew what kind of trouble that could lead to . . .

"You tell me!" He pounded the tabletop. "All I know is, more than half a dozen folks spoke to me after church. Said they wouldn't be able to come to the opening. The very same women who'd told me that they could hardly wait to have a dress-goods shop in town. Something happened to change their minds!"

"What did you hear?"

That question seemed puzzling enough to calm him down some. "Nothing, exactly. But I had that feeling—folks were talking about something they didn't want me to know." He scowled. "The ones who did speak to me were plenty clear. They're not coming to the opening, and from the way they were talking, they've no plans to become customers, either. Not a one of them would tell me why. And for every one who spoke to me, I'm betting there are others who think the same."

Word must have gotten around town about Hanna's encounter with Swenson. It didn't matter what had actually happened. The townspeople, most of them anyway, would assume that *she* was to blame, just as Mrs. Blake had.

Indecent. Sinful. Un-Christian. That was how they were thinking of her.

And they would not patronize the shop where such a girl worked.

She pressed her hands hard against her stomach. Not only had she been assaulted, but that same attack was being twisted to hurt Papa and the shop. The weight of the wrongness was crushing her; she didn't know whether to cry or scream curses or run to the privy and be sick.

Breathe. Breathe.

"You heard anything—any talk about us or the shop?" Papa asked.

"I've been home since yesterday afternoon," she said, careful not to lie. "I haven't seen anybody except Bess."

Papa was shaking his head. "I guess there's nothing for it," he said. "We'll just have to open as we planned, and see what happens."

His shoulders were hunched in what looked like defeat. Hanna was alarmed to see him like that. *I'd almost rather he were angry again.*

She groped for a thread of hope. What if she and Papa waited things out? Maybe the wave of gossip and rumor would ebb and eventually fade from everyone's memories.

But if people made up their minds that she wasn't respectable, they might force her to carry the taint for as long as she lived in LaForge. She and Papa would have to leave town to escape it.

۰٪۰

Hanna ate only two bites of her dinner. When Papa went upstairs for his Sunday afternoon nap, she put on her bonnet and went out the back door. The beginnings of a plan had come to her.

Miss Walters lived on Second Street, east of Main. Hanna did not have to walk up Main Street; she could get to the Walters place through the alleys. She reached the house and knocked on the front door, hoping that it would be Miss Walters who answered and not her mother or brother, with whom she lived.

"Hanna?"

Thankfully, Miss Walters came to the door herself. Distraught, Hanna cut short her greetings. "Hello, miss. I need to ask you something."

"Would you like to come in?"

"No—no, thank you, miss."

Miss Walters stepped outside. She led Hanna around to the back of the house, where there was a bench against the lean-to wall. They sat down side by side.

"Papa heard that—that people aren't going to come to our shop opening. And maybe not going to buy goods there at all."

"I'm sorry, Hanna."

She did not ask why, which meant that she had heard the whispers. Hanna felt ashamed even as she battled against the feeling.

"Miss, I wanted to ask if—if you thought it would do any good for me to go around town and—and call on people. On the women. To try to change their minds and get them to come to the shop." The thought of doing such a thing made her feel almost sick with misery. "I could tell them what really happened. It wasn't my fault—I swear it wasn't, miss."

"I believe you, Hanna," Miss Walters said quietly. She paused, then added, "It's not the first time that Mr. Swenson has been involved in—in unpleasant altercations."

Hanna inhaled sharply. "If that's so, miss, the ladies might . . . might listen to what I have to say—" She stopped, seeing misgiving in Miss Walters's eyes.

For a few long moments, neither of them spoke.

"If I were you," Miss Walters said slowly, "I think I would let things alone for a while." Kindly, she put a hand on Hanna's arm. "This may be one of those times when least said, soonest mended."

Hanna's head bowed as she shrank into herself. Miss

Walters was acquainted with almost every family in town and would surely know better than Hanna how they might react to her calling on them. "Yes, miss."

"I know it must be difficult, but I'm certain things will turn out for the best."

"Thank you, miss."

Hanna said her goodbyes. On the walk back home, she wondered what it would be like to feel certain that things would turn out for the best.

Hanna broke the Sabbath by working on the green dress. She would complete it regardless of what had happened, because Mama would have disapproved of leaving it unfinished. Odd—normally the prospect of a new dress would have been exciting. This one would forever be a reminder of failure. Even so, working was better than sitting still; being busy helped push the memory of the assault into a darkened corner of her mind.

On Monday morning, the day before the opening, Hanna answered the door to Bess's knock. But Bess did not step inside.

"I'm sorry," she said, her voice low and tremulous. "I'm not coming to work today." She looked at Hanna, her eyes full of regret. "It's not me, I swear. It's Ma. She—she says I can't work for you anymore. She didn't even want to let me come here to tell you, but Pa said I could."

Hanna stood very still—first in shock, then with growing anger. The Harrises had obviously heard about what happened. Mrs. Harris's reaction was entirely predictable. Mr. Harris had allowed Bess to come to the shop to deliver her message, but *not* to continue working. He, like Miss Walters, was sympathetic, but only to a point. They were in favor of fairness and justice as long as it wasn't too inconvenient or uncomfortable.

Mama, why aren't you here? I can do the sewing, but I can't fix anything else. It's too hard to do alone.

She sensed Mama's silent answer.

"Alone?"

Hanna waited, her head down, staring at her shoes.

Was that all?

Mama, please say something more . . .

"Hanna, please say something."

Startled, she looked up. Bess was still standing before her.

You're right, Mama. I'm not alone.

Mama had known the importance of helping other

people—*and* of accepting help from them. The missionaries. Miss Lorna. Papa, their customers, her friends. Maybe that was part of what it meant to be independent: learning when to be strong on your own, and when to be strong with the help of others.

"Bess, can I talk to you for a moment?"

BESS CAME INTO THE KITCHEN but politely refused to sit down. Hanna stood facing her.

"It's pretty clear that folks have heard about what happened Saturday. But they haven't heard the truth. They think that I misbehaved. Badly. So badly that they're not going to come to the opening. Or buy from our shop. It's just not right that my family's whole livelihood is about to be ruined. Because of lies."

"I'm sorry," Bess whispered for a second time.

"How sorry?"

Bess blinked.

"You say you're sorry that this is happening to us. Are you sorry enough to help?"

"But what could I do?"

A faint hope rippled through Hanna.

"I need the women in town to know the truth—that those men attacked me, and I wasn't misbehaving in any way. But I don't want the law involved, because then my father would have to be told."

She stared into Bess's wide blue eyes. "If I tried to convince the ladies, they wouldn't believe me. No, it's worse than that—they wouldn't even let me in the door to speak to them. But *you* could do it. They'd invite you right in. They'd listen to you, even the ones who would never give me the time of day."

"I'm not good at talking to strangers," Bess said.

"I didn't say it would be easy."

Silence.

"I want to help—really I do," Bess said, her eyes filling with tears. "I just don't think I can. What would I say to Ma?"

The ripple of hope was dissipating. *It's a hard thing, what I'm asking her to do. But somehow I have to get her to see that it's not nearly as hard as being ignored and spited and attacked and hated, and losing your business and your home . . . and the only real friend you've had in years.*

For if the shop proved unsuccessful, Papa would have to sell up and they would move on yet again.

She wondered what she would remember about their time in LaForge—the good things, she hoped. Those weeks at school, when it had been just her and Bess and Sadie studying with Miss Walters . . .

"Miss Walters." Hanna's own voice surprised her. "She could go with you."

Bess raised her head. "Do you think she would?"

"I don't know. I went to see her yesterday. She told me not to do anything—'least said, soonest mended.' But it took her a while to say that . . . Anyway, you could start by talking to her."

Bess seemed to stand up a little taller. "That much I can do."

All morning Hanna hoped that Bess would return during the noon hour to tell her how things had gone. Dinner came and went with no visit from Bess, and then the afternoon seemed to lengthen without end.

Hanna spent most of the day working on the dress: the last stretch of hemming, the piping on the sleeves, and twelve vexatious buttonholes. The only good thing about Bess's absence was that Hanna had more than enough to keep her busy. And, while she wasn't proud of it, she couldn't help the petty, spiteful thought that Bess had left her to do all the buttonholes herself.

When she had at last finished the hundreds of tiny knotted buttonhole stitches, she sewed on each of the twelve glass buttons, good and firm. Then she stood and stretched, rolling her shoulders. She reached up with one hand to rub her cramped neck muscles, but then remembered the bruises and lowered her hand slowly.

Don't think about it. Keep moving.

After she put the flatiron on the stove to heat, she worked on covering the lard cans. The blue cans were lettered with the words PURE LARD in white; their tin edges were rusty and the paint chipped.

She picked out a pretty but inexpensive pink-striped calico and cut from it six carefully measured rectangles. Once she had sewn a quick rough seam to join the ends of a rectangle, she could open out the fabric to form a cylinder about six inches tall. She slipped a cylinder over each can, then tied on a length of cream-colored ribbon.

The plants had done their part to perfection, blooming right on schedule. Hanna rearranged the window display. She moved the rack of fabric off-center to the left and placed the six rosebushes in their disguised cans here and there on the sill. Papa had screwed a metal hook into the ceiling of the window well, on the right-hand side. That was where she would hang the finished dress.

The lawn ironed up beautifully, the fabric smooth and soft. Hanna hung the dress on a hanger, and the hanger on the hook. Then she stepped back to look at the entire display. It was facing into the shop, as the window itself was still covered over with brown paper. She would turn everything to face outward in the morning.

The blue "sky" above, the lovely fabrics on the rack, the prairie roses in full bloom, and especially the green sprigged lawn dress . . . Hanna was so proud of how the window looked that she wanted to clap her hands like a child. *Mama would have loved it.*

But in the next moment, tears were wetting her eye-lashes. What if no one came to the opening? What if she and Papa were the only people in town who ever saw the display?

At least a dozen times, Hanna paced the length of the building, between the window at the front and the lean-to at the back, hoping to see Bess return. She waited for her friend until the sun had disappeared below the edge of the prairie.

Bess did not come.

If she had good news, she'd have been here by now.

"Good night, Papa," she said, the words stilted by the lump in her throat. Her insides felt hollow. If someone were to nudge her shoulder, she thought, she would collapse to the floor, crumpled like a threadbare rag.

Papa was still in the shop, sweeping, dusting, polishing, by the light of a lantern. He had already cleaned the whole place but was doing it again, as if buffing the woodwork until it gleamed would bring in the customers. She sensed that he, too, needed to keep moving.

He looked up and nodded at her, but did not stop working. "Good night, Hanna."

Hanna got into bed and turned on her side. She thought she might cry, but her eyes remained dry. She lay awake for a long time, bone-weary and heartsore. Eventually she heard Papa's tread on the stairs and the creak of the floorboards as he went to bed.

In the darkest part of the night, she thought of something she had forgotten to do. She rose, lit the lantern, and tiptoed downstairs. She found what she needed in the workroom, then fetched the dress from the window display.

Hanna unbuttoned the dress's collar. On the underside

of the collar near the right shoulder seam, she embroidered a tiny five-petaled lotus in pale pink thread. Then she rebuttoned the collar and smoothed it down.

There, Mama. Now it's finished.

She hung the dress in the window again and crept back upstairs. The night sky had lightened to gray by the time she finally fell asleep.

"Hanna! What's the matter—are you poorly again?"

Yanked from sleep by Papa's voice calling from downstairs, Hanna sat up so quickly that for a moment the room reeled around her.

"I'm fine, Papa," she called back. "What—"

"Then hurry yourself and get down here."

Mystified, Hanna dressed hastily. She rushed into Papa's room to look at the clock; it was a few minutes before nine. She couldn't remember ever sleeping this late before.

Then she heard an unfamiliar sound from outside. The window in Papa's room was at the front of the building, above the shop. She looked out the window and choked back a cry of astonishment.

On the sidewalk, there was a long line of people—a line that crossed the alley and went halfway up the next block.

Mostly women and girls, a few men. They were chatting cheerily, and those standing by the window were gazing at the display, pointing, nodding, smiling. Which meant that Papa must have taken down the brown paper and turned everything in the window well to face the street.

"Hey, Edmunds!" one of the men called out. "It's nine by my watch! You opening today or not?"

"That's right—it's nine o'clock!" someone else said.

As Hanna watched, Papa opened the door and went outside. "Yes, we're open," he said. "Come on in, everyone, and welcome."

Hanna drew back from the window, dizzy with disbelief.

Bess had done it. Somehow, she had gotten what looked like half the town to come to the opening.

Hanna hastened from the kitchen to the shop carrying two platters of cookies. Bess followed behind her more slowly so as not to spill the full pitcher of ginger shrub she was holding. Mrs. Blake and Ellie from the hotel had brought stacks of tin plates and cups for serving.

The shop was full of people; the bells on the doors were jingling almost constantly. Everyone was talking, looking at the goods, nibbling and sipping the refreshments. The button box was of great interest, as was the window display, with customers crowded around both. Papa took another pitcher of ginger shrub out to the sidewalk, where a group of menfolk had gathered. Hanna noticed that he was wearing his good boots, which gleamed from the polish she had given them.

Miss Walters greeted Hanna, then took Hanna's hands in hers and gave them a little squeeze. "Bess and I had a very interesting walk yesterday," she said quietly. "You were right, Hanna, to send her to me."

Hanna looked at her and nodded, not trusting herself to speak without tears.

Miss Walters smiled. "I'm thinking about a visiting dress. Will you show me the poplins?"

The raffle was a tremendous success. Papa called out the names to applause and exclamations of surprise and delight. Miss Walters won the needles. Mrs. Murphy, from the drugstore, won the button string. The posy of ribbons went to Ellie, who declared that she would wear them all at once, making everyone laugh. Hanna was especially glad that Ellie had won a prize.

Mrs. Wilson at the hardware store won the lace. The winner of the grand-prize sewing basket was Mrs. Schmidt, the pastor's wife.

Then Papa drew Mr. Grantham's name for the men's raffle and called him inside to claim his prize. More applause and laughter greeted him as he went to stand next to his wife.

Mr. Grantham, who owned the furniture store, had a

full mustache and muttonchop whiskers. Mrs. Grantham had a round girlish face and graying brown curls. Both were plump and pink-skinned.

Mr. Grantham looked at the card that Hanna had made. "Twenty percent discount! All right then, Wilma, you can order that dress you wanted."

"Whatever are you saying, Harold? Now that you've won the discount, I'm going to order two!"

The morning was not perfect. There were customers who greeted Hanna icily and spoke only to Papa. A few addressed her as they might a servant, tersely, without using her name. Still others said not a single word to her. But the overall sense of gaiety bubbling through the room helped her ignore any unpleasantness.

She and Bess stole a few moments together in the workroom.

"Thank you," Hanna said, her smile tremulous. It occurred to her that her family's fortunes had become tightly meshed with the Harrises'. Mr. Harris was the reason she and Papa had come to LaForge in the first place. Bess was helping keep them there. At the same time, Hanna was helping Bess by employing her . . . and perhaps in other ways, too.

"You're welcome," Bess said. Pause. "That was a fine idea of yours, for me to go to Miss Walters first. I couldn't have done it alone, and she—well—"

"She wouldn't have done it without you," Hanna finished for her. "When I saw that line of people outside the door, I could scarce believe it. How did you do it?"

"We made a plan," Bess said. "It took us a long time—the whole morning, and again after dinner. We laid out to say different things, depending on the person. I wrote them down and read them aloud until I knew them nearly by heart. That was Miss Walters's idea, to make it almost like a reading lesson. She said that if I knew well what I wanted to say, I wouldn't be as nervous saying it. She was right."

They had begun by telling the ladies the truth: that Hanna was fetching lard cans from the hotel when the two men attacked her. "I said I'd seen for myself the marks on your shoulder. Then we would remind them of the times that Mr. Swenson has gotten into trouble before, because of drink. That part was always easy for them to credit."

Bess reported that with some of the women, she and

Miss Walters would talk about the shop. "Mrs. Grantham and Mrs. Murphy, and a few others—the ones who wear their Sunday best even during the week. I told them that I'd seen the dress goods, and how lovely the shop is, and how good you are at dressmaking." Bess grinned at the memory. "Really, they didn't need much persuading."

Other women proved more difficult to convince. Bess frowned. "It was strange. None of them seemed to have any problem believing that those men were at fault. But still they made excuses."

She glanced away, her face growing pink. Hanna guessed what Bess did not want to say: that certain women were reluctant to patronize the shop because Hanna was half-Chinese.

"Some people are just . . ." Hanna trailed off, unsure how to finish her thought.

"Rotten eggs," Bess finished for her.

A moment's pause, and they both burst out laughing. After they caught their breath, Bess went on. "At Pastor Schmidt's, Mrs. Schmidt mentioned that your father tithes. So then we told the ladies that staying away from the shop would mean less money for the church. That's what I told

Ma, too. And Mrs. Blake said—" Bess stopped, her expression suddenly aghast.

"It's all right," Hanna said. "Whatever it is, I'm sure I've heard it before."

Bess nodded. "She said she didn't know that Chinamen could be Christian."

Hanna had indeed heard that before. "I didn't know they couldn't," she replied.

A brief silence. Hanna had saved the hardest part for last. "Your ma didn't come," she said.

"Oh! Ma got all the washing in off the line and had to iron this morning," Bess said blithely. "She said she'll come one of these days."

Hanna knew that ironing was not the only reason for Mrs. Harris's absence. But it seemed that Bess wanted to think the best of her mother, and Hanna could hardly blame her. Mama could not have been perfect, but that was how Hanna remembered her.

Mothers and daughters . . .

She had a blinding flash of insight then, about her encounters with the Indian women. During their first meeting, Wichapiwin could have observed that no one except Papa was making the journey with Hanna. Wichapi-win might well have surmised that Hanna was motherless.

I thought it was me being kind, when really she was the one making sure that I didn't feel left out.

The opposite of how Mrs. Harris had made her feel. She wondered if she would ever get the chance to thank Wichapiwin.

"Do you think your ma will let you keep working here?" Hanna asked.

Papa had taken no fewer than *seven* orders from women who wanted dresses made up. More than enough work to keep Bess on until she had to leave to teach school. Hanna had already begun designing the dresses in her head, and every one of them would have a tiny pink lotus embroidered somewhere on the inside.

"Yes," Bess said immediately. "She let me come to the opening. She even told Pa to give me a ride here in the wagon."

Perhaps Mrs. Harris's reason for allowing Bess to continue working at the shop had more to do with family income than anything else. But Hanna wondered if the change of mind might one day lead to a change of heart as well.

THE PARTY BEGAN TO quiet down toward midmorning, as the guests departed to see to preparing dinner for their families. With only a few people left lingering in the shop, the bells tinkled as the door opened yet again.

Sam Baxter entered with his little sister, Pearl.

"Hello, Hanna," he said.

"Hello, Sam. Hello, Pearl." Hanna was surprised to see him—and doubly surprised by how glad she was.

"I've brought Pearl to visit your new shop," Sam said.

"I figured it wasn't the other way round," Hanna replied with a smile.

He laughed. "I'm not much for dresses," he teased back.

Pearl was looking around, her eyes large with amazement. "Can I see that?" She pointed at the button box.

"Of course," Hanna said. "You take your time. I'll be right back."

Hanna hurried into the workroom. She opened one drawer, then another, and found the length of red ribbon she had put away weeks earlier.

Back in the shop, Hanna held out the ribbon. "Here, Pearl, this is for you," she said.

Seeing the joy on Pearl's face was by far the best moment of Hanna's day.

"A ribbon!" Pearl exclaimed, reaching eagerly. "Will you tie it for me, miss?"

"Of course," Hanna said. Pearl turned around, and Hanna began tying the ribbon to join the ends of Pearl's two little braids.

A pang of yearning surprised her.

Because Mama had been sick for nearly as long as Hanna could remember, another child in the family had never been a possibility. As Hanna tightened the red bow, she realized for the first time what a sister or brother would have meant to her: someone with whom she could have shared memories of Mama.

Someone else who would have been half-and-half.

Pearl pulled one of her braids to the side so she could see the cheerful red bow. Over her head, Sam and Hanna exchanged smiles.

"I heard you graduated," Sam said. "Congratulations."

"Thank you," Hanna said.

Pearl returned to her perusal of the button box. Sam beckoned Hanna surreptitiously, and they stepped a few paces away.

"I'll be back soon, without her," Sam whispered. "It's her birthday next month, and I was wondering if you could make some doll clothes for her."

"Such a lovely idea!" Hanna exclaimed. What fun it would be to design and make little doll clothes. "Bring the doll with you, if you can. Or at least measure her? And bring Pearl for a visit whenever you like."

That bright smile of his. "I will," he said. "It'll be something for her to look forward to."

Me, too, Hanna thought as she waved goodbye to them. *I'll look forward to seeing you again, Sam Baxter.*

Could she learn to enjoy his company without thinking too far ahead? It now seemed possible—as if, in a single stroke, the success of the shop's opening had altered her view of the future. She might well be in charge of the shop in the years to come, but today it seemed more than enough to know that for the next few weeks, she would be sewing.

She had been wrong earlier, when she thought that her work as a seamstress would endear her to all of LaForge. There would always be those she would never win over, no matter how many fine dresses she made.

But she realized now that she no longer needed the approval of the whole town. She had a home with Papa, work that she loved, and a few good friends.

Tea with friends is a feast for the spirit.

Mama had never said those words. Hanna had thought of them herself that very moment. *It's what I would say to her, if she were here now.*

Hanna spent the rest of the week measuring customers for their dresses, helping them choose patterns and fabrics, drawing sketches of changes to the patterns. Then she and Bess began pinning, basting, cutting, stitching. She went to bed early almost every night, exhilarated but also worn-out from the long hours in the workroom. Often she fell asleep when there was still light in the western sky.

Staying busy during the day helped ward off memories

of the assault; being exhausted at bedtime kept away the nightmares. On the Saturday after the grand opening, she was in the workroom pinning a pattern piece when a thought struck her so hard that she jammed a pin into her finger without even feeling it.

What would she do when she saw Mr. Swenson again?

It was bound to happen. Maybe not for days or even weeks, but sooner or later, she would be walking down Main Street, and he would be there.

Should she avoid him—cross the street, change her route? But what if he saw her first? Perhaps she could make her face blank. Or better still, ignore him altogether.

She tried to imagine walking past him, her head high, utterly unaffected by his presence. But the possibilities for disaster seemed endless. Her knees might buckle. She might faint or get sick or start to cry. She could already feel her stomach churning.

Breathe, she told herself sternly.

She filled her lungs deeply, once and then again. She took a handkerchief from her pocket and pressed the fabric against the pinprick of blood on her left middle finger. As she bent again over her work, she still didn't know what to do.

At least she had asked the question, which had not occurred to her earlier because she hadn't been ready. It was the first step. Before there could be answers, there had to be questions.

She decided to make every effort not to run errands alone, at least for a while. It would be easier to ignore the man if someone else was with her. She also thought about warning other girls and young women to steer clear of Swenson. Bess would surely be willing to help with that. And Miss Walters might have other suggestions.

Hanna already knew that she would never be able to forget what Swenson had done to her. She had to learn not to let him do it again and again in her head and in her dreams. For that, she would need to draw strength from other people—the people in her life who cared about her. Bess. Miss Walters.

Maybe even Papa, one day, someday.

On an evening a week after the opening, she was in bed dozing off when Papa's voice woke her.

"Hanna? Come give me a hand—I need your help."

What could he want at this hour? she wondered.

Thickheaded and rusty of voice, she called down to him. "Do I have to get dressed?"

"No. Just put on a wrapper."

She grabbed Mama's old plaid shawl to drape around her shoulders and went down the stairs in her bare feet, still trying to rub the grogginess from her eyes. The sun had set, leaving behind a blue-gray twilight.

Papa met her in the kitchen. "Close your eyes," he said.

She obeyed, of course, but couldn't help saying, "Papa?"

"Would you do as I say this once?" His words were curt, but in his voice she heard more amusement than exasperation.

He took her by the hand and walked her to the far end of the workroom.

"There," he said. "Now, a little to your left . . ." He guided her another step or two. "All right. Open your eyes."

Hanna blinked. In the dim light, her vision was clouded at first.

Then she gasped at the shadowy image in front of her.

A ghost? A mirage?

But she looks so real—even her shawl . . .

She moved her lips soundlessly. *Mama?*

"Well? What do you think?" Papa's voice rang sudden and loud in her ear.

He stepped forward, and at last, she realized what she was seeing.

Her own reflection in a full-length mirror, with Papa behind her.

The mirror was a long oval of glass with a smooth beveled edge, mounted on a hinged oak stand. While not as big as Mama's wall mirror, it was in one way even more useful: The glass could be tilted to alter the viewing angle, to focus more on the lower or upper half of the body.

She turned to give Papa a hug. He dropped a quick kiss on the top of her head. "Who ever heard of a dressmaker's shop with no mirror?" he said, smiling.

"You'll have to repaint the sign," she said. "It's not Edmunds Dress *Goods* any longer. It's Edmunds Dress *Shop*."

"Yes, boss," he said, heaving a mock sigh.

They laughed together. Then she faced the mirror again.

Hanna had viewed her reflection many times, in shop windows and puddles of water, and in the small looking glass. But it had been years since she had seen her whole self with such clarity.

Nor had she known how much she had come to resemble Mama. Beautiful Mama.

"So you like it?" Papa asked.

Her reflection nodded at them both.

"Yes, Papa," she said. "It's exactly what I need."

Author's Note

I WROTE HANNA'S STORY as an attempt at a painful reconciliation.

Among the most beloved of my childhood books were those written by Laura Ingalls Wilder. I read them all many times—so often that to this day, fifty years later, I still know countless phrases and passages by heart. As an adult, I have met numerous immigrants and children of immigrants who, like me, adored the Wilder books. My theory is that we saw them as providing a kind of road map to becoming American. We believed—mistakenly, as I would later learn —that if we made maple-snow candy and a nine-patch quilt and a corncob doll (and named it Susan) just as Laura had, we might, one day and somehow, be as American as she was.

Of the eight Wilder books published during her life-time, the last four are set in De Smet, South Dakota. As a child, I would lie in bed night after night, imagining that I, too, lived in De Smet in the 1880s, and that I was Laura's best friend.

I had to do some pretty fancy mental gymnastics to get myself to De Smet during that era. There were no Koreans in the US at the time; the first group of Koreans to immigrate here would not arrive until the early 1900s, and they would land in Hawaii, not on the continent. There were, however, thousands of Chinese immigrants, most of them on the West Coast. They had arrived in two main waves: during the Gold Rush years of the 1840s and '50s, and to help build the transcontinental railroad in the 1860s. Census records of 1875 show a population of Chinese in Dead-wood, South Dakota, about 350 miles west of De Smet.

There were certainly people in China at the time who were half-Korean. So during those nighttime imaginings, I became an Asian girl living in De Smet—a Chinese girl with some Korean blood.

The Wilder books were set in the Midwest, the very region in which I lived. The stories I invented were a pre-internet version of fan fiction. They were usually rosy romances. In Wilder's *These Happy Golden Years*, Laura is courted by Almanzo. They get engaged and finally marry. Meanwhile, I was being courted by Almanzo's handsome friend, Cap Garland.

Even at the height of my passion for those books, there were parts that I found puzzling and distressing. The character of Ma was the most problematic. Her values of propriety and obedience over everything else seemed to me both misplaced and stifling.

And Ma hated Native Americans. In several episodes throughout the series, she expresses that hatred. While I could not have articulated it at the time, I harbored a deeply personal sense of dismay over Ma's attitude. Ultimately it meant that she would never have allowed Laura to become friends with someone like me. Someone with black hair and dark eyes and tan skin. Someone who wasn't white.

The racism that Hanna confronts is largely autobiographical: I have faced almost exactly the same incidents of racism depicted in the book. Whether outright hostility from strangers or thoughtless microaggressions from closer to home, such encounters are frequent, even daily, occurrences for me and almost every black or brown person I know. Racism is, however, not a series of incidents. Rather, the incidents are evidence of deeply ingrained states of personal bias and institutional injustice.

It wasn't until I was well into adulthood that I learned something of the true history of the devastating effect that westward expansion had on Native Americans. Likewise, the true histories of other people of color here in the US are largely missing from our educational curricula and our national consciousness. The dearth of stories centered on the struggles and contributions of people of color has resulted in the pervasive, harmful, and sometimes even deadly attitude that we are not as fully human as whites. Those stories are of vital importance to every single one of us living in this country. To ignore them is an incalculable loss, because learning their truths makes us stronger and more capable of facing the challenges in our communities.

In *Little Town on the Prairie*, Pa takes part in a blackface minstrel show. The show is an obvious delight to Laura and the other members of the all-white audience. While both Laura and Pa in the books are often at odds with Ma's mistrust of Native Americans, the portrayal of blackface evinces no such qualms.

There are those who argue that Wilder cannot be

faulted for that attitude because she was "a product of her time." Others point out that this is no excuse for treating any members of the human race as "lesser" — that there have been people in every time and place who have risen above the limitations of standard social mores. While I agree with the latter sentiment, I also can't help pondering which of our current and widely held attitudes will be found lacking by future generations. Is our vision any clearer than that of our forebears?

Fans of Wilder's work will, I hope, be able to recognize where I have both acknowledged and challenged her stories. The town of LaForge is modeled on De Smet, the locations of the homes and businesses based on the map that Wilder herself drew and labeled. The Harris family is partly inspired by the Ingallses; Dolly Swenson might remind readers of Nellie Oleson. As part of the research for this book, I visited De Smet, South Dakota, and Mansfield, Missouri, the two main sites for Wilder pilgrimage.

(A note to those who love the television series *Little House on the Prairie:* I may have watched one or two episodes as a child, but no more than that. I can clearly remember my fury on seeing that the actor playing Pa *had no beard,* and that alone was enough to cause me to boycott the show.)

In Chapter 5, there is a mention of a plant called "yansam" in Chinese. The Korean word is "insam"—ginseng in English. Korean ginseng has been prized throughout Asia for centuries for its medicinal qualities, used for everything from memory loss and fatigue to heart conditions and diabetes. As of this writing, scientific studies are inconclusive as to ginseng's effectiveness.

Other parts of the book are based on historical events, including the Los Angeles riots of 1871 (Chapter 2); the mentions of the Sioux treaty with the US government (Chapters 1 and 21); the Gold Rush at Pike's Peak in Colorado (Chapter 2). The one historical figure mentioned in the story is James Harvey Strobridge, construction foreman of the Central Pacific Railroad (Chapter 20). Initially reluctant to hire Chinese men, and always ruling them with an iron fist, Strobridge eventually grew to admire them as workers. "The Chinese are the best workers in the world! They learn quickly, do not fight, have no strikes that amount to anything and are very clean in their habits. They will gamble and do quarrel among themselves most noisily—but harmlessly." (James Harvey Strobridge, quoted in Erle Heath, "From Trail to Rail," *Southern Pacific Bulletin,* XV, Chapter XV, May 1927, 12.)

To research the scenes where Hanna encounters Wichapiwin, I visited the Pine Ridge Reservation and several other important Native sites in South Dakota, including Wounded Knee and the Crazy Horse Memorial. At Pine Ridge, I was privileged to have as my guide Donovin Sprague, Lakota author, historian, and teacher. Mr. Sprague helped me track down a braid of prairie turnip, which I soaked and cooked just as Hanna does in the story. I also attended an intertribal mini-powwow in Fargo, North Dakota, where I learned more about Native life, both historical and contemporary. I was especially moved by hearing the powerful honor songs.

A note on terminology: I have used the words "Sioux" and "Indian" because that is what people in Hanna's time would have used. Had the white population in Dakota Territory been interested, they could have learned that Wichapiwin and her companions were members of the Ihanktonwan tribe, Dakota speakers of the Oceti Sakowin Nation. The Ihanktonwan (Yankton) Reservation is south of De Smet; Hanna and Papa would have driven nearby on their way to the town.

I also chose to include a few lines of Dakota dialogue. I felt strongly about including those words in an effort to counteract previous generations of innumerable children's books that have never depicted or even acknowledged Native languages, and the stereotypes of Hollywood that reduced Native communication to grunts and pidgin. Today, many indigenous nations are working hard on language revitalization programs.

In a letter to her daughter, Rose, in April 1921, Laura Ingalls Wilder wrote about greeting an African American man at a meeting of her local farm loan association: "Our colored member was there and when he was introduced to me I shook hands with him which nearly paralyzed some of the others." (Laura Ingalls Wilder, *The Selected Letters of Laura Ingalls Wilder,* ed. William Anderson [New York: HarperCollins, 2016], 28.)

I like to think of that handshake as a clue to how Wilder might have reacted to *Prairie Lotus*. The Little House stories were written years after that letter; her awareness had not grown enough for her to deal with the harmful scenes in her books. But I hope she might have been open to learning how her work affected a young Midwestern Asian girl who grew up to be a writer.

Prairie Lotus is a story I have been writing nearly all my life. It is an attempt to reconcile my childhood love of the Little House books with my adult knowledge of their painful shortcomings. My wish is that this book will provide food for thought for all who read it, especially the young readers in whose hands the future lies.

Acknowledgments

SO MANY PEOPLE to thank. That is in itself a blessing.

Throughout my childhood, my father, Ed Park, took me to the library, where I first encountered the Little House books. My mom, Susie Park, taught me to sew, knit, and embroider when I was a child, and I have vivid memories of the clothes she made for me and my siblings.

I am grateful to the citizens of a number of Native Nations for sharing their insights and wisdom. Andrea M. Page (Hunkpapa) and Mary Blackcloud Monsees (Hunkpapa) provided the transliterations of the Lakota language. Andrea also gifted me with my second-ever braid of timpsina (timpsila in Lakota). In addition to spending the day with me on the Pine Ridge Reservation, Donovin Sprague (Minneconjou), author, tour guide, and historian, read the manuscript and sent helpful comments. Cynthia Leitich Smith (Muscogee), Dawn Quigley (Turtle Mountain Band of Ojibwe), Joseph Bruchac (Abenaki), Melody Staebner (Turtle Mountain Ojibwe), and Darlene TenBear Boyle (Crow Agency Apsaalooke and Turtle Mountain Ojibwe) gave me general information and advice with generosity and kindness.

Ruth Hopkins, journalist, activist, and tribal judge, Sisseton-Wahpeton Lake Traverse, read the manuscript, advised on the changes from the Lakota language to Dakota, and gave me comments that were especially valuable. An example: Because Wichapiwin and Hanna cannot communicate verbally, their exchanges take place mostly by gesture. In several instances, I had depicted Wichapiwin pointing with her forefinger. Hopkins wrote, "The Oceti Sakowin (Sioux) consider pointing with one's finger to be rude. Instead, we point with our lips, or simply motion with our hand."

To me, this is a perfect example of the adage, "You don't know what you don't know."

Alice DeLaCroix provided assistance with sewing details. Kimberly Brubaker Bradley gave me advice on horses. Jim Armstrong was my railroads expert and volunteer cold reader. Anna Dobbin answers my endless tech and grammar questions.

In Mansfield, Missouri, Anna Bradley, assistant director of the Laura Ingalls Wilder Home and Museum, gave me a tour and graciously answered my many questions.

In regard to all of the above, any errors in the text are my responsibility.

Marsha Hayles has critiqued drafts of all my books, including this one, and almost always responds within a few days—even for an entire novel. Other writer friends held my hand and listened to me whine about this story. I thank everyone at the Society of Children's Book Writers and Illustrators and We Need Diverse Books for their support, and for the opportunities and challenges of serving on their advisory boards.

Dinah Stevenson pulled my first manuscript from the slush pile in 1997. This is our eighteenth book together, all for Clarion Books/Houghton Mifflin Harcourt. I am the most fortunate of writers to have an editorial relationship of such longevity. With this book, as with the others, she guided me to the story I was trying to write all along.

More thanks to the team at Houghton Mifflin Harcourt: Amanda Acevedo, Lisa DiSarro, Jessica Handelman,

Eleanor Hinkle, Anne Hoppe, Catherine Onder, John Sellers, Tara Shanahan. Andrea Miller designed the book's interior, which I find both attractive and easy to read. Seeing Hanna brought to life by jacket artist Dion MBD, combined with Sharismar Rodriguez's lovely jacket design, made me weep for joy.

Ginger Knowlton has been my agent for more than twenty years, a relationship I cherish more than I can ever express. Thanks also to the whole team at Curtis Brown, Ltd., for always being in my corner.

My husband, Ben Dobbin, has always allowed me the time and space to write my books. For this one, I needed more of both than ever before, and he gave me those gifts with grace.

Jackie Woodson, Laurie Halse Anderson, Leah Henderson, Olugbemisola Rhuday-Perkovich, Ellen Oh, Renée Watson, An Na, Namrata Tripathi, Daniel Nayeri, Meg Medina, Grace Lin, Tammy Brown, Jim Averbeck, Ed Porter, Pat Cummings, Melissa Stewart, Cynthia Leitich Smith, Dr. Sarah Park Dahlen, and many others are among the friends and colleagues who have taken the time to talk to me about race, diversity, and inclusion. I ask their patience and forgiveness, as I still have so much to learn: My goal is to make new and different and better mistakes every day.

Finally, I thank my readers—of all ages, but especially the young readers. It is an honor and a privilege to be able to write for you.